I0552309

Her Clockwork Heart

By

Dena Garson

Her Clockwork Heart
Copyright © 2017 Dena Garson
Edited by Heather Long

Cover art by Emmy Ellis ~ Studioenp (www.studioenp.com)

Originally published by After Glows Publishing in 2017

All rights reserved.

This book is a work of fiction. Names, characters, businesses, places, and incidents are the products of the author's imagination or used fictitiously. Any resemblance to actual persons, living or dead, or actual events is entirely coincidental.

ISBN: 978-1-945075-15-5 (print)

DEDICATION

As always, for my boys.

ACKNOWLEDGEMENTS

I want to give a big "Thank You" first to Cameron Allie. Because of her and our sprinting sessions I was able to finish not only this book but also *Vordol's Vow*. On time. Without losing my mind or stress eating. Cameron – you were the kick in the pants I needed the last few months! Thank you!

I also need to give Lauren Smith squeezing "Thank You" hugs for answering my seemingly endless questions about historical England. Yes, some of them were stupid and I probably focused way too much on minutia but she answered them without laughing in my face. Lauren - I'll buy you cheese fries at our next lunch.

1

NATHANIEL Dennison rubbed the spot between his eyes where his head throbbed. He'd been reading files for the last three—he glanced at his pocket watch—correction, four and a half hours. After all that time, he had more questions than answers.

There was a connection between the disappearances he'd been asked to investigate. He just couldn't put his finger on it.

He took a deep breath. He had to be missing something. The blank lines of his notebook mocked him. When had he ever come up with so few clues on a case?

Only with the Mastermind.

He scowled at the stack of files he'd reviewed. The Mastermind had all members of the Royal Intelligence Office on edge, investigators and officers alike. They had been searching for the men behind the political unrest and outright attacks on the royal family for almost three years. No one could pin down who was behind the espionage and hints of treason. His Royal Highness had become increasingly insistent on answers.

Not that Nathaniel blamed him at all. No one in the RIO did. They wanted answers almost as much as he did. Smoke would be easier to catch.

With a sigh, he straightened his mess and tucked his notebook away in the breast pocket of his coat. He reached for the lamp to douse the light but paused when something banged against the wall of the records room.

Most of the RIO staff had left for the evening. By now he should have the offices to himself, with the exception of the security officer who patrolled through the night. But he would have sworn he recently heard the officer's footsteps echoing down the hallway.

As silently as possible he exited the file room. At the door to the records room, he paused and listened. There were shuffling sounds, like boxes being moved about, as well as odd clicks and whirls. Almost like a clock with a gear out of alignment.

"No, not that one," someone whispered on the other side of the door.

Was that a woman's voice?

"Hurry. We don't have much time."

Again, no response to the whisper, but the clicking sounds multiplied.

Nathaniel checked the lock on the door. It had been opened. The intruder either had a key or a considerable talent with locks. The locks used at the RIO were unusual and gave even the most experienced lock picks trouble.

He pulled his derringer from his pocket then as quietly as possible turned the door handle. The last click of the latch set off a flurry of activity inside the room.

So much for a stealthy entry.

He positioned himself against the wall, yanked the door open, and leveled his gun on whatever he found inside the room.

Some kind of insect jumped off one of the file cabinets onto Nathaniel's outstretched hand and pinched him.

"Ouch!" He shook his hand and tried to dislodge the bug, but it moved too fast. "What the bloody hell?" He bellowed when the bug ran across his arm then down his chest and leg to the floor.

"Don't hurt her. She won't hurt you," a woman called out from the other side of the cabinet. "Nid, get over here." Papers were shuffled and more clicks came from that side of the room.

Her voice was familiar. Nathaniel lowered his gun but kept

it at the ready as he made his way to the other side. As he crept forward he looked left and right for more bugs. "Who is that and what are you doing in here?"

More shuffling of papers. A drawer slammed shut. The woman whispered, "Squeaks. Hopper. Get in."

Nathaniel stepped around the end of the cabinets and leveled his gun at the person crouched next to the cabinet. He blinked in surprise at the woman who looked up at him. "Trixie?"

Beatrix Wadeworth froze with her hand extended to two small creatures that resembled a toy mouse and small rabbit. "Nathaniel?" She started to stand, then paused and scooped up the toys and slipped them into her pocket. "I uh…" She glanced behind him toward the door.

He took two steps forward and grabbed her by the arm. "Don't even think about it."

"Wh… what are you doing here?" she asked breathlessly.

"I work for the Royal Intelligence Office so I'm allowed to be here but you're not." He tightened his grip on her arm. "What are you doing here?"

Two of the bugs ran up his arm. He tried to brush them off, but only managed to hit one of them.

"Nid, it's okay." She nabbed the one shaped like a spider. "Come here."

"What are those?" They looked like bugs, but the whirling noise and clicks gave away the fact that they weren't.

"They're my, well…" She shrugged and dropped the one she'd taken off his arm into the pouch at her waist. "They're my friends."

"Friends?" One of her other toys scratched at his pant leg as it tried to climb it.

"Oh, sorry." She reached for the creature but stopped when her face drew too close to an area of his anatomy that no proper young woman should be near.

"I'll get it." He released her arm, slid his pistol back into its holster, then plucked the tiny mechanical insect from his thigh. He examined it for a moment then dropped it into her open palm. The strange assortment of metal gears and parts were shaped to resemble a scorpion.

"Thank you," she murmured.

"How many more of those do you have?"

"I only brought five of them with me."

He opened his mouth to say something then shook his head. "You can't be here."

"What the deuce is going on in here?"

Trixie's eyes widened with alarm. Nathaniel groaned. Great, the security officer had found them. "I was just finishing up for the night, Adam," Nathaniel told him.

"No one other than RIO personnel is allowed in the records room," Adam said sternly.

"I'm sorry. That's my fault," Trixie said.

Nathaniel tried to grab her but she swatted his hand away.

"You see, we were supposed to have dinner tonight, but someone…" She gestured at Nathaniel. "Forgot." Then she looked back at the guard. "He gets so forgetful when he's working. I insisted that if he had work to finish, then I should at least sit with him."

"That doesn't explain why you're in the records room," Adam said stiffly.

Nathaniel opened his mouth to say something but Trixie cut him off.

"Oh, pish posh." She waved one of her dainty hands at the guard. "I wasn't about to be left alone in that boring old office. I need to make sure he finishes whatever he needs to do so that he has plenty of time to take me to dinner." Her eyes grew wide. "Oh wait." She faced Nathaniel. "Is that why you said I needed to stay in your office? Because I'm not allowed to be in here?" She looked back and forth between the guard and Nathaniel in mock surprise.

"Something like that," Nathaniel said through gritted teeth as he slipped his pistol into his pocket.

"That's right, miss. No one other than authorized personnel is allowed in the records room."

"Oh, no. I thought you were just trying to avoid me." Her

eyes grew round and filled with tears.

Despite his annoyance, Nathaniel couldn't help but be impressed with Trixie's display. If he didn't know better, he would have sworn she'd had some kind of training for the stage.

"I'm so sorry. I didn't mean to break any of the rules."

His breath lodged in his chest when she closed in on him, practically grasping the lapels of his coat.

"I didn't mean to get you into trouble. We haven't seen much of each other lately and I just wanted to stay with you. Please don't be cross with me." She suddenly released him and turned to the guard. "Please don't turn him in. He didn't do anything wrong. Not really. It's my fault. I followed him in here. He really did try to make me stay in his office. You're not going to tell his superiors, are you?"

She turned her attention back to Nathaniel. "I'll explain to them what happened. Surely they'll understand." She drew one finger across her lashes, as if to wipe away a tear.

"I'm not sure—" Nathaniel said, momentarily distracted by the delicate floral scent that teased his senses when she had pressed against him.

"Please don't get him into trouble." She took a few steps toward the officer. "I'll go back to his office right now. I promise. I won't move a muscle from the seat. Just please don't tell on him."

"Now, Miss. Just calm down." Adam told her in a placating manner.

"I'll go right now."

She tried to brush past Adam but Nathaniel rushed forward and grabbed her by the arm. "How about if we leave so Adam can get on with his patrol?"

"No harm done, Miss." Adam said. "I'm sure you didn't mean to break the rules."

She turned large, pleading eyes on him. "No, I didn't. Truly."

"My apologies, Adam," Nathaniel said. "I should probably take her to dinner. I've made her wait longer than I should have."

"Yes, sir." He tipped his hat to Trixie. "Good night, Miss. And just remember, if you visit again the Inspector there knows where you are allowed and where you're not."

"I will remember that."

Nathaniel tugged her toward his office.

"And thank you," Trixie called back to the guard.

When they reached his office she said, "Oh, my, that was close."

He glared at her. "You have no idea."

2

HOW did she end up in this situation?

Nathaniel Dennison. Of all the people in the world to catch her doing something nefarious, why did it have to be him? Not only was he the son of a Viscount, he was the man she thought she might marry someday.

Of course, someday never came.

Because of that other day. The day her parents disappeared and her world had fallen apart.

She cringed. As if her family's reputation had not been damaged enough. What ever would he think of her now? Now that she had stooped to breaking into intelligence offices.

He hadn't spoken a word since they left the security officer. He'd simply dragged her to a tiny office where he'd collected his hat and cane. When she'd tried to ask a question he'd cut her off with a growl and a warning to not say another word until they were outside.

Clearly he was cross with her. She lifted her chin. She would risk his displeasure and so much more if it gave her the information she needed.

Once they were outside, away from the building, Nathaniel stopped in the middle of the road and faced her. Surprised by the suddenness, she skittered to a halt as gracefully as she could. "What's wrong?"

"What's wrong?" he bellowed. "Everything about you being in there is wrong. What—" His hand balled into a fist then opened again. "Why—" The muscle in his jaw jumped. "I just don't—"

She blinked at his partial statements. "You don't what?"

"Bah." He turned on his heel and marched down the street.

Perhaps she should just run in the other direction and get away from him. That would be cowardly. She had gotten herself into this mess. She would get herself out. She took a deep breath then hurried to catch up with him. "Are you all right?"

"No. I am not all right. I have just lied to one of our security officers and that does not sit well with me."

"Actually, I did the lying, you just didn't correct what I said."

The look he gave her from the corner of his eyes should have burned her on the spot. Instead, she decided that his stern and disapproving attitude suited him remarkably well. She grinned which made him frown even more.

When they reached the end of the block he steered her to the right then across the street.

"Where are we going?" she asked.

"Someplace we can talk privately."

She skidded to a stop. "Just where were you planning to take me?"

He paused. "No place immoral, if that is what you're worried about."

"I wasn't until you mentioned it."

He stepped closer and his tone gentled. "I wouldn't do that to you, Trixie." He pushed a lock of her hair behind her ear.

"You wouldn't be the first to assume that my morals had slipped." She shrugged. "After all, you did just catch me doing something rather illegal."

"True, but I also assume that you have a very good reason for it."

"I do."

"And I plan to hear all about it." He took her by the arm. "But not out here."

He slowed his pace to one that she could easily keep up with. They stopped at a small tavern on the next block. He opened the door for her and motioned her inside.

Inside the darkened foyer an older man with a curled moustache greeted them. "Good evening, Mr. Dennison. Wonderful to see you."

"Good evening, Charles."

"Table for two?"

"Yes, please. Preferably a quiet, out of the way booth."

Charles dipped his head. "Right this way, sir."

He frequented a tavern so much that they knew him by name? Perhaps this hadn't been a good idea.

They followed the man to the back of the room. While the front part of the tavern bustled with patrons crowded around a bar their table was blocked off enough to minimize the noise and distractions. The high walls of the stall made it a private nook.

"Will this be adequate for your needs this evening?" Charles asked.

"Perfect. Thank you."

Charles left the list of the evening's entrees on the table. "I'll let Loretta know you're here."

Trixie slid into her seat then adjusted her skirt while Nathaniel sat across from her. "Come here often?" she asked.

"Not as often as I'd like. The owner and I are old friends. We went to university together."

"Ah." At least he wasn't known because of his frequent patronage.

The serving girl came by and took their orders. As soon as she left, Nathaniel asked the question she had been dreading. "What were you doing in the records room?"

A weight settled in her gut. She owed him an explanation since he hadn't turned her over to security but that didn't mean she had to tell him everything. "The short answer is that I was searching for something."

"That is far too obvious of an answer. What were you searching for?"

"Anything that might tell me what happened to my parents."

He frowned. "I thought they died when their airship crashed in the jungle."

"So did I." She tamped down the wave of grief that always surfaced whenever she thought about her parents' disappearance.

He lifted one brow. "But you don't any longer? What changed your mind?"

"We received a message telling us father was alive and if we wanted to ever see him again we needed to retrieve Father's journal from the Royal Intelligence Office."

"Who was the message from?"

He wasn't going to like her answer. In truth, she didn't like it either. "I don't know."

"But you did as they asked?"

"Peter and I did."

"Peter? Peter wasn't with you." Nathaniel frowned again. He leaned forward in his chair and growled in a low voice, "Tonight wasn't your first break in was it?"

She cringed. "It was the first time I've been in the *London* office."

"You've been in other RIO offices?"

"Yes. Three before tonight."

He blinked in surprise. "How is that possible?" He didn't give her a chance to answer. "Why would you take that kind of chance? You had no way of knowing for certain if the person behind that note was friend or foe. They could have been sending you on a wild goose chase or setting you up to be arrested."

She said a silent prayer of thanks that they were in a public house so he couldn't shout at her. "You're right, but we couldn't take the chance. If Father really is alive we didn't see any other way of finding him."

His hands clinched into fists. "Why didn't you go to Scotland Yard and ask for help?"

"The note warned us not to."

"Of course it did, but you still could have gone to them and quietly asked for assistance."

She leaned forward in her chair and hissed, "Don't you think we tried? Peter talked with a friend who frequently works with them on cases and asked what we should do. He advised there would be little the constables could do to help and that the potential publicity would likely only draw unwanted attention back to the family. Not to mention word would likely get back to whoever sent the note."

Nathaniel cringed.

They paused their conversation when the serving girl arrived with their drinks. As soon as the girl left Trixie continued. "The first time we went in to one of the offices we calculated we had at least a small chance of getting in and out without anyone noticing."

He leaned back in his seat and folded his arms over his chest. "I'd be most interested in knowing how you managed to pull that off."

She shrugged. "Peter's friend told us about the records room and how they filed things. After a little training with a, um…" She cleared her throat. "An acquaintance with a talent for breaking into secured places, Peter and I felt it was our best shot. Between the two of us and the automata we were able to get in and out fairly quickly."

"Automata." He glanced at her reticule. Nid, her mechanical spider, hovered at the opening, seemingly watching their exchange. "Did you find what you were looking for?"

"My father's journal? No."

"So you were being set up for something," he surmised.

"We don't think so. Every office we searched had files on father. We gathered whatever information we found and brought it home to study. Originally, we planned to return everything after we'd read it, but now we can't be sure that information wouldn't be used against him if we did find Father."

"Each of the offices had files on him?"

She nodded as she took a sip of wine. "Most had the same basic information—his background and family connections—but one had details of the crash."

"I can't believe that Peter let you do something like this on your own. What is wrong with him?"

She cringed.

"And why did you go to the other offices first instead of starting with this one? I could have helped you from the start."

"We planned to leave the London office for last because of its close proximity to home. We thought we were far more likely to be seen or recognized here. It just wasn't worth the risk before."

"You couldn't find the journal at any of the other offices so this was your last hope?"

"Oh, no. I found notes in the Plymouth office files that hinted an inspector from Edinburgh had found a journal at the crash site."

His teeth were gritted when he asked, "Then why did you need to break into this one?"

"I haven't been able to make arrangements to travel to Edinburgh just yet and I wanted to see what information they might have here before I did."

"And Peter was fine with you doing this without him?"

"Don't be ridiculous." She encouraged Hopper to come out of her bag. "He didn't want me involved at all. But once he saw how much faster the automata and I could get in and out he relented."

He shook his head. "I think I need a drink of something stout before we finish this conversation. Excuse me for a moment."

How did she get into this pickle? She slumped against the back of the booth. She was sitting in a tavern with the former love of her life. After he caught her doing something extremely illegal.

It had been three years since she last saw him. The Crenshaw's mid-summer festival had been a glorious evening. She spent most of the day and night at Nathaniel's side. They danced, ate lunch and dinner together, and simply enjoyed a warm, carefree day. But her bliss quickly turned into tears when she returned home and learned her parent's airship had been reported as lost, with no survivors. She and Peter had immediately packed and left for the mysterious continent of Africa to do what they could to find their parents.

When she returned five months later, she learned Nathaniel had taken an assignment in Paris and would be gone for an undetermined time. There had been no letters from him. No words of condolence. Nothing. And it had hurt deeply.

But, given the lies that quickly spread about her father and how he'd supposedly been working with a disreputable firm to sell illegal goods and information, she hadn't been surprised. Most of her supposed friends turned their backs on both her and Peter.

Despite her bruised heart, she kept a watchful eye for Nathaniel's return to England, but had not reached out to him. Somehow their paths hadn't crossed before now. Granted she no longer moved in the same social circles. As a matter of fact, she did very little socializing. And no dancing at all. Not since... well, him.

Strange that she hadn't noticed that before now.

3

WHEN he returned to their table after sending a note off to one of his colleagues he found Trixie lost in her thoughts. Her fingers toyed with one of her mechanical pets but her mind was clearly elsewhere.

"Forgive me. I just needed a moment to clear my head," he told her as he took his seat.

"Understandable." She gave him a sad smile. "This evening probably didn't go the way you planned."

"No, it did not."

Her eyes widened in concern. "I do hope you haven't had to cancel other plans."

"No. My plans for the evening were simple. Finish reviewing the files related to the case I'd been working then have a quick supper at home." He shrugged one shoulder. "I live a simple bachelor's life."

"Well good." She blushed. "I mean, I'm glad I'm not keeping you from any other engagements." She took a sip from her glass. "So might I ask about your connection to the Royal Intelligence Office?"

"I joined the RIO about four years ago. I've been steadily working my way up since."

"You never said anything about working for them. I thought you had a commission with the navy."

"The RIO is a special branch of the navy. We don't tell many people who we really work for."

"Does your family know?"

"Mother does."

"But not Sophie?"

He shook his head. "She thinks I am still in service for the navy." He shrugged. "Less for her to worry about."

She frowned. "How? Is the RIO more dangerous than the navy?"

"Depends on how you look at it." He latched on to the opportunity to question her further. "Speaking of worried siblings, should we send a note to Peter letting him know where you are?"

She looked down at the automaton crawling across her fingers. "No, that won't be necessary."

"Surely he will be expecting you home by a certain time. Especially after your escapades tonight." He tipped his glass in her direction. "And just so you know, I will be having words with your brother about either of you getting involved in this on your own. Most especially about him letting you do this on your own."

"He doesn't know about tonight."

Her words came out so softly he almost missed them. "What do you mean? I thought you said the two of you had been going into the offices together and he realized you were faster at it."

She nodded and finally met his gaze. "That's true. But he had nothing to do with tonight. He doesn't know I did it."

Nathaniel clenched and unclenched his jaw. "Explain."

"Peter went missing three days ago."

Her words hit him like a slap to the face. His mind quickly sifted through all of the files he'd been reviewing about missing people. The possibility that Peter might be yet another of the casualties filled him with dread. "Tell me everything you know."

"That isn't much."

"Tell me anyway."

She took a deep breath. "The last time I saw him was Thursday."

"Where?"

"At the Panhurst offices. I left early because I needed to run by the market for a few things. Peter said he wanted to work on something in father's lab and would be home late."

"Do you know what he was working on?"

"No. He and Father were just alike. Always tinkering with something or another. I never have been able to keep up with their ideas much less which they were most interested in. That changed from day to day."

The serving girl interrupted them to deliver their dinner orders. Once everything had been situated and the girl left, he prompted Trixie, "Go on. You were telling me about Peter."

She sampled her soup then nodded as she patted her mouth with her napkin. "Yes. Like I said he left the office early on Thursday and from what I have gathered from the housekeeper and the delivery boy who often runs errands for Peter, he remained there overnight. The next day is what I cannot get firm answers on." She pushed the food around on her plate. "Basically, no one can account for his whereabouts after about one o'clock in the morning."

"When did you realize that he was missing?"

"I noticed Friday morning but I didn't worry until later that afternoon."

"What did you do in between?"

"Mostly went about my normal day. I did tell our housekeeper that I hadn't been able to find Peter and asked her to send word if he came home. I also sent one of the men to the club Peter frequents and a couple other places he might have visited to see if anyone had seen him. Then late Saturday, I searched father's laboratory myself to see if he left a note or clue to his whereabouts."

"I take it you didn't find anything?"

She shook her head. "Nothing to raise any concern."

"If your father's lab was the last place he was known to be, do you mind if I take a look tomorrow?"

"I don't see what harm that would do but what do you hope to find?"

"You said you searched for a note from Peter. I'm just…"

He took a moment to wipe his mouth with his napkin while he carefully chose his words. "I'm curious to know if he left the lab under his own power or if someone helped him."

She crumpled the napkin she clutched. "You think someone kidnapped him?" Her voice trembled ever so slightly.

"I think it is within the realm of possibility." He hated creating more worry for her but she was far too intelligent to be handed half-truths.

"I'd already considered that. I just didn't want to admit how much of a possibility it really was," she confessed.

He lay his hand over hers. "I'm not saying that is what happened."

She nodded. "I know. We won't know until we see all the facts. Or until we find Peter."

He squeezed her hand.

"Can we talk about something else for a bit?"

"Certainly." He pulled his hand back. "Did you have something in mind?"

"Why did you never write to me after Mother and Father disappeared? Of all the friends I lost, you were the one I missed the most."

He reeled back in surprise. "For months, I didn't know where you were or how to reach you. I didn't even know what had happened for almost a week when the rumors began to surface. By then I figured…" He paused. "By then I figured that I had been mistaken in my estimation of our relationship."

"What do you mean?"

"I thought if the details of your life had been relevant to me then you would have told me what was going on."

Her eyes widened. "I did."

"You did, what?"

"I left a note for you that night. I asked one of the maids to have it delivered the next day."

He shook his head. "I never received anything from you."

"But I…" She looked bewildered. "You never received my note?"

"No."

She slumped back in her chair. "I sent one in care of your mother since I didn't know where your place was. It was hastily written and probably very messy, but I did think you should know what little I did know at that time."

"You sent it to Mother's?" Understanding dawned. His mother had not approved of his attachment to Trixie. She'd always hinted he could do far better than the daughter of an inventor. It wouldn't surprise him if she conveniently lost the note.

"Yes. I asked Lilly to deliver it first thing the next morning."

He tapped his finger on the table in annoyance.

She smiled sadly. "I didn't feel right leaving without telling you something. I know we didn't have any kind of understanding, but I counted you as one of my friends and…" She pressed her lips together and looked away. "I remember being sad that I wouldn't be able to dance with you again at the Cunningham ball the following weekend."

So she hadn't run off without a second thought for him. He'd spent the better part of a year thinking he'd been mistaken about their relationship. "You returned to London while I was in France, didn't you?"

"That's what I heard." She sampled the greens on her plate. "Once Peter and I were permitted entrance to some of the social events, that is."

He frowned. "That had to be a hard transition for the two of you. The ton can be vicious when there is any hint of scandal."

"A hint is all it takes to close a great many doors in this town." She took a deep breath. "But we had father's business to keep us busy. Between the legal and financial issues we had to face when we returned as well as the general running of Panhurst, there were more important things to worry about instead of which balls we didn't receive an invitation for."

He snorted. "The years I spent abroad were a bit of a Godsend for me. Mother became a little too aggressive in her search for a suitable wife for me and I needed the time away from the ballrooms."

"Why did you go to France? I understood that you were visiting a distant cousin?"

"That's Mother's story. In truth, I was on assignment for the RIO."

Her surprise quickly turned into amusement. "You weren't spying on anyone, were you?"

"While I cannot discuss that case even today I will say that it was an eye-opening experience and taught me how deep political connections run."

"Intriguing."

They spent the remainder of dinner catching up. Nathaniel shared a few of the funnier experiences he'd had aboard. She told him of the things they'd been doing at Panhurst. How she and Peter somehow managed to keep their father's company from going bankrupt after his disappearance and supposed links to crime.

That alone was impressive.

After they'd finished dessert Nathaniel ask in a low tone, "After successfully breaking into the RIO, what were your plans for the remainder of the evening?"

She flicked a loose curl over her shoulder. "I had originally thought of toasting my success from the bell tower of the church."

"How hedonistic of you."

She placed her hand on the table next to her toy rabbit and encouraged it to climb on. When it did, Trixie ran her finger down its back as if petting a real animal. The rabbit nudged the tip of Trixie's finger with its nose.

"They're very... animated," he remarked.

"Father was quite proud of his creations."

"Your father made them?"

"Yes. It was something he worked on for several years, but didn't perfect until right around..." Her hand froze in mid-air. Her gaze locked onto his. "Until a few months before he disappeared."

Nathaniel leaned forward and took a harder look at the spider sitting not far from his own hand. "I would think that there would be no less than a dozen investors who would love to know how he did it."

Their gazes met. A piece of the puzzle clicked into place.

She tucked the rabbit into her bag. "I believe it is getting late."

He scooped up the mechanical spider and handed it to her.

"Thank you." After adding the spider to her bag she paused. "I didn't thank you for not turning me over to your security guard or having me arrested."

"Don't thank me just yet." He stood then offered her his hand. "I never said there wouldn't be repercussions."

She eyed him warily. "What kind of repercussions?"

He gestured for her hand. She finally set her fingers on his open palm and slid out of the booth. "I considered taking you over my knee for acting so rashly."

Her mouth fell open and her cheeks turned pink.

"Instead, you'll have to put up with my assistance in finding Peter."

"That's not much of a punishment."

"You say that now, but after two days of me telling you that you are forbidden from breaking into any more offices or putting yourself in danger, you may change your mind."

Her barely audible "harrumph" did not reassure him that she was in line with his thinking.

4

THEY left the pub and strolled to the end of the block. There Nathaniel hailed a hackney and directed the driver to her home. She marveled at how the ride could be both comfortable and uncomfortably silent.

As they drew closer to her front door he finally asked, "What are your plans for tomorrow?"

"Peter and I used to split our time at Panhurst, but since he's gone missing, I'll need to be there each day."

"Fine. I'll meet you there."

"For what?"

"I'll go by the RIO in the morning and pull any files we have on your father and his disappearance."

"Would you look for information on Peter also?"

"Yes, although I'm reasonably certain we don't have anything on him. His disappearance is so recent I would have heard about it if anyone had been assigned to investigate." He tapped the side of his thigh. "Would you mind very much if I updated my superior on his disappearance?"

"I don't..." She chewed her lip. "Do you think that is wise?"

"I can tell him in confidence." He glanced out the window of the carriage. "He has far more contact with the inner workings of the government than the rest of us. He often makes connections before others can even process the information. He could be a powerful ally."

"But the note said—"

"I understand your worry, but he isn't the sort of person to let confidential information slip."

She took a deep breath. "Very well. If you think he could be helpful then I'll trust your judgement."

"Thank you." He took her hand and squeezed it. "May I ask one other thing of you tonight?"

"What's that?"

"I know you're anxious for information on your father, but will you promise me that you won't go out again this evening?"

Her lips twitched. "I promise to go in and straight to bed."

He raised a brow at her omission.

"And to not go out again this evening."

"Thank you."

When they stopped in front of her home he got out then helped her down. "One moment," he told the driver. With her hand still in his, he escorted her to the door.

"I'm sorry we had to run into each other in the manner in which we did," she told him. She gazed into his eyes. "But I am glad to see you again."

"I am, too." He raised her hand to his lips and placed a kiss against her knuckles.

Tingles ran down her arm and through her body at the touch.

"I will see you tomorrow morning. It won't be early, but I expect I can be there before lunch."

"All right," she stuttered.

He reached around her and opened the door for her to enter. "Sweet dreams."

"You too."

He gave her a wink and waited for her to close the door. As soon as the latch clicked into place, she slumped against the door.

"Everything all right?" The housekeeper asked from the doorway to the kitchens.

"Yes, Mrs. Ellison. Everything is well. Better than expected actually."

"Is there word of Peter then?"

"No, I'm afraid not. But my evening was pleasantly unsuccessful."

"I, uh… I see."

Trixie waved her back to her room. "Not to worry. I'm in for the night. I threw the bolt on the door and I'll just see myself up to bed."

"Will you be wanting breakfast in the morning?"

"Just tea and toast." She headed to the stairs.

"Good night then."

"Good night." Trixie floated up the stairs, still giddy from the renewal of her acquaintance with Nathaniel.

Were they friends again? It felt as if they were. Hoping for more than friendship might be premature and even dangerous. Yet, it bubbled to life inside of her.

As she readied herself for bed, she relived their conversation as well as every look and touch. The Nathaniel she'd dined with tonight was a more mature, more confident version of the young man she knew before. Not that he had been wild before. He'd always been dependable and loyal, but something had changed. Perhaps, like her, his experiences had curbed his youthful exuberance.

By the time her head hit the pillows, she wore a sappy grin knowing she had something to look forward to for the next day.

~ * ~

So much for a pleasant day.

Trixie rubbed her head where it had begun to ache. Keeping the scowl off her face had become a taxing effort.

"Miss Wadeworth, I'm afraid our investors would feel more comfortable finalizing this transaction with your brother."

Trixie cast a glance at the pudgy man who struggled to keep pace with her. "I understand your concerns, Mr. Chamberlin, but Peter is still out of the country."

The Panhurst man in charge of shipments, Devadas, accompanied her as she led Mr. Chamberlin and three of Mr.

Chamberlin's associates through the crowded shipping docks. They paused long enough to observe the bustling crewmen removing shipments from newly arrived air vessels or loading out bound ships scheduled to depart. She had hoped to prove to the stuffy old men that her family's company was still in good hands, despite her brother's absence.

"You said he had to leave unexpectedly?" Mr. Chamberlin asked.

"I'm afraid so." She turned her face away so none of the men could see the pain their question caused.

"Are you sure he hasn't been persuaded by Thackery & Company to enter into another deal and he is too cowardly to admit it?" the man with the thin moustache asked.

Trixie stopped in her tracks and glared at the man who dared to ask such a question. "Certainly not. If we... er, I mean Peter, had decided to contract with a different company you would have been notified accordingly. To do otherwise would be underhanded and cowardly. Something neither of us would tolerate." She looked each man in the eye to make sure they grasped her sincerity.

"It's just—"

"It's just what, Mr. Chamberlin?" She raised one brow in question. "You are unaccustomed to doing business with the fairer sex? Even though you know Panhurst Air is a family business?" She let out an exasperated sigh. "You've worked with us long enough to know that Peter and I both have been helping my father with every aspect of this company since we each learned to tally accounts." She pointed her umbrella at the tall thin man in the dark suit and added smugly, "I was only nine at the time."

"You may know enough to handle things while you brother takes a short break, but that doesn't mean you are capable of making decisions such as this."

Trixie glared at the tall man with the top hat. His condescending attitude made her want to toss the contract in their faces.

"Miss Wadeworth," Mr. Chamberlin tried to pacify her.

"We simply must have that contract signed by the end of the month."

"And your signature will not suffice," one of the other men in the group added.

"Fine. Leave the document with me. I will personally deliver it to Peter for his review." She shrugged one shoulder. "I had planned to go and visit him on another matter anyway."

The men of the group exchanged glances. "Very well." The man with the top hat unlatched his case and removed a packet of documents." He looked down his nose at her. "I hope we don't have to explain the confidential nature of this document. The information in it should not be shared with anyone outside of the principle owners of Panhurst Air."

She tipped her head at Devadas, letting him know she wanted him to take the document.

Devadas reached in from behind the man and gently took the packet from his hand. The man's discomfort from the sudden appearance such a large man made her smile.

"Gentlemen, if that is all. I do have other business to attend to." She waved one of the passing crewmen over. "Jeremy will show you out."

"But Miss Wade—"

"Good day, gentlemen." With that note of finality, she turned on her heel to return to the shipping office. Devadas fell in step behind her effectively blocking any further attempt to delay her departure.

When they were well out of earshot Devadas came along side of her. "I don't think you'll be able to keep that group at bay much longer."

She grimaced. "I don't either."

"It's a shame they don't know who really runs this business."

She snorted. "We're all better off if they continue to think Peter in charge. You see how they reacted to my offer to sign the contract myself."

"I don't understand why they are uncomfortable. You have legal provision to do so. Every bank in London knows it."

"Yes, but knowing it and allowing it are two different things. Women should be seen and not heard. And God forbid they engage in any form of business."

In a lower register of voice Devadas said, "We need to find Peter soon."

Her heart twisted. "I know."

"Miss. Wadeworth, there is a gentleman waiting in the office for you. A Mr. Dennison?" Mrs. Anderson, her office attendant, told her. "He said you were expecting him."

"Yes, thank you." To Devadas she said, "That's the friend I told you about that might be able to help find Peter."

"Shall I come with you?"

"No, that won't be necessary. I'd much rather you make sure that Jeremy herded those bankers out of the bay without incident. And then would you mind checking with Jerald on the Dublin flight? I think we may need to find a different ship if their cargo has increased as much as Mr. Robinson hinted."

"Yes, of course." He cast a glance toward the office.

"I will fill you in later. I promise."

She thought he might argue with her but he finally gave her a brisk nod then turned to do as she asked.

Devadas had been a blessing in disguise for the last two years. Peter met him on one of his many trips abroad. When he saved Devadas' life he had pledged his loyalty. Peter's offer of a job in London only furthered his loyalty to Peter, and now, by extension, to her. He was one of a small handful she knew she could count on without hesitation.

She found Nathaniel waiting for her in the front office. His broad shoulders encased in a well-tailored jacket looked out of place against the backdrop of dockworkers and pilots, yet he somehow managed to blend in. He'd always had a classically debonair look but now it balanced delicately with a quiet lethal confidence. A bubble of warmth burst inside of her when he caught her gaze from across the room.

His lips lifted in a smug grin as if he could read her thoughts.

"Good morning, Mr. Dennison. Thank you for coming this morning," she said when he drew closer.

"My pleasure." He tucked his cane between his arm and his chest and reached for her hand. Once again the kiss he placed on her knuckles sent a ripple of awareness through her. "I trust you slept well?" He asked with just a hint of a grin.

"I did. And you?" Despite the butterflies in her belly she managed to sound calm.

"I did, thank you." He presented her a box sitting atop a small stack of files, loosely tied with string. "I brought you something."

"Oh?" She took the package from him. "May I open it?"

"Perhaps in your office?" he suggested.

"Right this way." She gestured to the door she had come through then led the way to the stairs. She and Peter had taken over the offices that faced the docks so they could keep an eye on the operation. It also gave them a degree of privacy from the hustle and bustle of the front office yet kept them within easy reach should a problem arise that they needed to handle.

She had barely set the box on the desk when Mrs. Anderson appeared in the doorway. "Shall I bring tea?"

Trixie looked to Nathaniel, who nodded his agreement. "Yes, please," she told the older woman.

After Mrs. Anderson left, Trixie gestured to the box. "May I?"

"Go right ahead." He took a seat in one of the chairs near the window.

Giddy to be getting something when it wasn't even Christmas, she reached for the box. It was too small and light to be files from Nathaniel's office. What else might he be bringing her? She pulled the string and opened the lid. Inside was an assortment of pastries. The smell of butter and chocolate wafted up and made her mouth water. "Are those what I think they are?"

"Mr. Henderson's specialty. I remembered you used to be quite fond of them."

"Oh, it's been ages since I've had one." She shot him a questioning look. "The bakery closed after he retired."

"He did but my butler and he are cousins. We are often

treated with surprise batches. Fortunately, this was one of those days."

"And you were willing to share with me?"

"Of course."

She clasped her hands together in delight. "Oh, you are a gem." She reached for one of the flaky delights then closed her eyes as she breathed in the scent then took a bite. "Oh my. May I assume you've already had your fill this morning?"

"Of course."

"So you won't think ill of me if I don't share?"

He chuckled. "Not at all."

5

WATCHING her enjoy the pastry ended up being more of an erotic display than he'd expected. He'd forgotten how she tended to immerse herself into experiences. Now he was sitting across from her with an uncomfortable bulge in his pants.

He got to his feet. "Why don't you show me around? I've never had the opportunity to explore the inner workings of an airship company."

"All right." She pointed to the files sitting on the corner of the desk. "Let me lock those up. I don't think either of us want them laying around for just anyone to find."

"Agreed."

She unlocked one of the desk drawers, set the files inside, relocked the drawer then dropped the key fob back into her skirt pocket. She gestured to the door. "Shall we?"

"After you."

She tipped her head and led the way out of the office and out onto the main part of the docks. There were three ships in various states of readiness. Her in-depth knowledge of not only the ships themselves, but of their cargo and shipping schedules impressed him. More so, her ability to interact comfortably with so many people of varying backgrounds —mostly men— impressed him more. She seemed perfectly at ease, almost energized, in a world where most women would not only be lost but possibly fearful.

Everyone they passed acknowledged her in some way, either with a greeting or a simple tipping of the hat. Some of the saltiest dock personnel treated her with respect and genuine fondness. He, however, received more than one questioning glance and even a couple of scowls probably meant as warnings.

They ended their tour at a sizeable storage building not far from the main office building. "This is Father's laboratory," Trixie explained.

"Ah." Nathaniel examined the building, assessing it for how quickly someone could escape without detection. There were only two doors —one of which had a heavy metal cage over it— and all of the windows were close to the roofline, nearly two stories above street level. Despite it being a shipping area, none of the crates or storage containers were stacked near the building.

"Did you find anything of interest?" she asked when he returned to her side.

"It's a relatively open space. Nowhere to hide." He pointed his cane in the direction of the outer fence. "However, it isn't far to the street. A carriage could easily wait on the other side for a fast exit."

Her brow furrowed. "True."

"Let take a look inside."

She nodded then pulled the key from her pocket to unlock the door.

The door had been made of heavy oak and had no windows and the locks were of sturdy construction. There were obvious signs of weathering and use, but no marks to make him think the door had been attacked in any way. Once inside Trixie sent two of her automata to trigger the lamps. The windows provided some light but most of the perimeter remained in shadows without lamps.

The first part of the building appeared to be mostly a dressing room. A couple of jackets hung from hooks on one wall. A pair of mud coated boots sat on the floor below them alongside a pair of men's shoes. On a nearby shelf lay a few neatly folded pants and shirts.

"Are these Peter's clothes?" Nathaniel asked.

"Mostly. He and father both kept extra clothing here in case they soiled their own." She smiled sadly. "Mother used to complain about father tracking grease and oil home. I think he kept old things here to wear while working."

There were stacks of newspapers in one corner. Above it were shelves of glass jars containing canned food and what appeared to be dried meat and candies.

She led him into the main part of the laboratory. Tables lined both of the longer walls and held an assortment of parts and tools. Some parts had been assembled into things he couldn't quite identify. The center of the room had been filled with sturdier worktables and metal racks.

Lamps were scattered throughout. Some affixed to walls, others on tables. At the far end of the building a metal staircase had been attached to one wall and led to metal catwalks that crossed over the main floor in the shape of an H. A few chains hung limply from the catwalk as if waiting to provide support for some new invention.

"Where does Peter do most of his work?"

"Over here." She led him to a desk along the larger wall.

The desk had stacks of documents in one corner. An ink well sat nearby along with a couple of well-used pens and pencils. Nathaniel flipped through the documents but nothing caught his eye. In actuality, it seemed to be a batch of unrelated papers. "Did your brother keep a journal?"

"Of course."

"Do you know where he keeps it?"

"I should think it would be here." She approached the desk. "Or possibly at home." Her voice lacked conviction.

He strolled through the rows of tables and tried to imagine what Peter might have been doing the night he disappeared. The things further back had a thin layer of dust. It made sense that his current project, or projects, would be located closer to the front entrance.

"Anything stand out to you?" she asked.

"Nothing conclusive." He frowned as he scanned the space again. "Nothing appears out of place. Nothing is broken or thrown about as if a struggle occurred. But in truth, the area feels… staged."

"Staged? In what way?"

"Almost too neat and orderly. Yet, nothing appears to be in progress." He gestured toward the back. "Except for the things back there that haven't been touched in some time."

She frowned and moved closer to the main worktable. She looked from there to the side tables then to the desk she said her bother used.

"Unless your brother is only interested in academic theories and research, then I believe he and whatever he has been working on are missing."

"Let me check one other thing," she murmured. She pulled her key fob from her pocket and hurried to a chest next to the wall. She started to unlock the chest but stopped. "Someone has broken the lock."

Nathaniel joined her at the chest. "You're right."

She pulled the broken lock off and opened the chest. With a groan she said. "They're gone."

"What are?"

"Peter's old journals."

"You mean notebooks he'd filled or used up?"

"Yes. They're gone. So are Father's."

"I thought you said you hadn't been able to retrieve your father's journal?"

"We haven't yet. His current journal is what we hoped to find at the RIO." The lid slammed shut when she released it. "Father kept his old journals here. Peter too."

"Ah."

"This just gets more and more cloudy," she murmured.

"Not really." He helped her stand. "I see it as one more piece in a large puzzle. Soon we'll be able to see the whole picture."

"I hope you're right."

"Of course I'm right." He winked at her.

Their gazes met. That old connection he'd always felt whenever he'd been with Trixie drew him closer. The temptation of being alone with her was more than he could bear any longer. He took her hand and pulled her toward him.

She didn't resist.

Ever so slowly he lowered his head and pressed his lips to hers. Gently. Teasing. He only wanted a sampling. To see if she still tasted the way he remembered.

Her lips parted on a gasp then her hands came to rest on his chest. Instead of pushing him away as she probably should, she sagged against him. He wrapped his arm around her back and deepened the kiss.

A hint of chocolate lingered on her lips. Whatever flowery soap she used permeated his senses and made him want to get lost in her. But this was not the time for that. Nor was it the place.

He eased away from their kiss but was pleased to see a dazed, almost drunkenness in her eyes when she finally opened them. "We should…" He cleared his throat. "We should probably get back to the office."

She blinked. "I, uh… yes." She glanced at his chest, where her hands were splayed out. "That would probably be best." Yet, she didn't step away.

Not that he was in hurry to release her. "Someone might come looking for you," he softly reminded her.

She drew herself upright. "Yes. Of course." She took a step back, then turned away.

He reached for her hand before she could fully withdraw. "We will finish this another time," he promised.

She gave him a jerky nod.

He gathered his cane from where he had left it on one of the tables then led the way to the door. He held it open so she could pass through then waited while she locked it.

"Perhaps luncheon is in order?" she asked.

"Yes. I find I am rather famished." He gave her a wink then offered his arm.

6

THEY enjoyed a late lunch at a place she frequented before returning to the Panhurst offices. She consulted with Mrs. Anderson on a couple of business items, then led him up to her office again.

"You said you kept the files you found at the other RIO offices, correct?" Nathaniel asked.

"That's right."

"I don't supposed you have them here, do you?"

"As a matter of fact I do."

"I should very much like to read what you found. Perhaps I could do that while you read these?" He gestured to the files he had brought with him. "Since I cannot permit you to keep these."

"Why can I not keep them?"

Her incredulousness made him grin. "Because we have a process. I had to check these out in my name. If they are discovered missing, I will be the first person the records keeper would contact."

"Very well." She shot another look of irritation his way before going to the file cabinet in the corner. Using a key dangling from the fob hidden in her skirt pocket, she unlocked the cabinet and pulled out a lockbox at the back of one of the drawers. With a different one, she unlocked the box and removed a small stack of documents.

He marveled at the number of keys she carried.

"This is everything I found." She pushed the stack across

the desk to him.

"That's not very much."

"Believe me, I know." Regret tinged her voice. "Oh," she said when she reached down to close the drawer. "What is this doing in here?" She took a notebook out.

"What is it?" he asked.

"I think it's one of Peter's journals." She opened the front cover. "It is." She glanced down into the open drawer. "But why would he have put it in here?"

"Do you usually keep that drawer locked?"

"Yes."

"Did he know that?"

"Of course. It's where I keep the Panhurst account books. He is the only other person with a key."

"Perhaps he wanted to make sure that journal was kept some place safe."

"He has locking cabinets in the lab. Why wouldn't he use his own?"

That was a good question but he didn't like the any of the answers he came up with. "We just saw that one of his storage lockers had been tampered with. Perhaps he knew there was some danger of his things being taken."

"He never mentioned anything."

Fear for Trixie's safety inched higher. "It's possible he didn't want to put you at risk by telling you."

"Maybe so." Her voice trailed off.

"May I?" Nathaniel pointed to the journal.

"I suppose." She handed the book to him.

He thumbed through the pages. The dates were recent and the entries looked like what you would expect for daily journaling. Trixie stared off into space for a few minutes before turning her attention to the files he had brought her. He wished he had words he could offer her for comfort, but nothing short of answers to Peter's whereabouts would help.

He pulled his seat closer to the corner of the desk so he could sift through the papers. As they worked, he found it much harder to concentrate in her office than his own.

Between watching the different expressions crossing her face as she read the information and the interruptions from various port personnel, including a small fire out in the rubbish pile, he had only made it through half the stack. Normally he could have read a half dozen complete reports and case folders by then.

The interruptions didn't seem to bother Trixie. She answered questions without losing her place or her temper. And she still managed to question him about details she found in the files that he might have missed had she not brought it up.

When he finished reviewing the information she had collected, he began reading Peter's journal. Instead of private thoughts, the pages held recounts of discussions with people he knew, new ideas, or results of experiments.

As they worked, the sun began to set and the dockworkers left for home. The port and the offices below them lapsed into a hollow quietness.

They worked together in a comfortable silence where only the occasional ruffle of paper or the squeak of a chair could be heard. In the back of his mind he wondered why she had never married.

Originally, he assumed it had been because of her parents' disappearance. But now that he had seen just how deeply she was involved in the family business, he wondered if there were more to the story. She was well above the age of majority. Some of the matrons of the ton would even consider her "on the shelf."

Weren't all young women in a rush to marry? In his experience, family encouraged a dash to the altar. With a suitable man, that is. Perhaps he should ask her why she remained unattached.

A creak of wood on the stairs outside the office drew his attention.

Trixie raised her head from where she had been reading. He gestured toward the sound to silently ask if she knew who might be coming upstairs.

She shook her head in answer.

Nathaniel gestured for her to duck out of sight next to one of the cabinets. Then he swiveled out his chair and pressed himself against the wall in the shadows so he could assess whether the person on the other side of the door was a threat. As he moved into place he pulled his pistol from his pocket. He hated that Trixie could potentially be spotted right away by whoever came in, but he needed to know what threats she might have hanging over her. If Peter had indeed been abducted against his will, it was possible she could be in danger too.

The handle of the office door rattled then the door slowly opened inward. A boy's head poked through the opening and swiveled in each direction. Curious what the boy wanted, Nathaniel remained hidden.

The boy crept to the desk and riffled through the documents on the desk. As soon as he reached for Peter's journal Nathaniel slammed the door closed. "You looking for something?"

The boy jumped. "No, sir. I, uh…" His eyes darted around the room.

Trixie came out of her hiding place. "What are you doing in here?"

"I believe this young man was attempting to relieve you of a personal item or two." Nathaniel stepped closer to the boy while blocking his exit.

"I was not!" The boy glanced from him to Trixie and back. "I was just hoping to find a few sweets." His face lightened as if an idea had just occurred to him. "To take to me mum and sister. I didn't mean no harm."

"How did you get in?" Trixie asked.

"Weren't hard. Loads of places to slip in without no one noticing." The boy shrugged. "At least for someone like me."

"Someone like you how?" Nathaniel asked.

"Plain. Easy to miss. Not very big." He jerked his thumb toward the area of the docks. "Not like some of the blokes working down there."

"And you were just looking for sweets?" Nathaniel allowed his doubt to come through in his question.

"All the way up here? In a locked building?" Trixie tacked on.

Nathaniel leaned one hip against the desk and tapped one corner of the book. "Were you hoping to find sweets inside the pages of a book? That's an odd place to look."

"Well," the boy went on, "you never know what you mind find."

Nathaniel and Trixie exchanged glances.

Trixie went to the cabinet near the desk. "What's your name?" She asked as she removed a tin.

"They call me Mouse."

"Mouse." She tossed a piece of candy to the boy. "What does your mother call you?"

"Mouse."

Nathaniel stifled a chuckle.

"What were you really doing in here, Mouse?" she asked.

The boy glanced at Nathaniel.

"We aren't going to call the Bobbies. But I need to know what you were doing here and who might have sent you." She tossed the boy another piece of candy.

He popped the second one in his mouth. "Don't guess it can do no harm."

"Did someone send you or are you working alone?" Nathaniel asked.

"Nah. Some bloke came around night before last saying he'd give a ten pence to anyone who could find a book for him."

"What kind of book?" Trixie asked.

"What bloke?" Nathaniel asked at the same time.

"He just said it would be about this big." The boy demonstrated length and width with his hands for Trixie. "And that it would have a lock that you couldn't miss." Then he looked to Nathaniel. "Right proper gent, he was. About your height. Wore one of those new hats I keep seeing the uppers wearing now."

"That's not much to go on," Trixie mumbled.

"Oh, and he had a red beard." The boy stroked his own chin for emphasis.

"That we can use," Nathaniel said.

Trixie tossed the boy another candy when he looked meaningfully at the canister she still held.

"What did this man say for you to do with the book if you found it?" Nathaniel asked.

"Said I should take it to the barkeep at the Angel's Folly."

Trixie tossed him another piece of candy.

He caught it then asked, "Can I go? No harm done."

Trixie looked at Nathaniel.

"I'll walk him out."

The boy tipped his hat to Trixie and gave her a charming smile. "G'nite, Miss."

"Oh, Mouse?"

Both the boy and Nathaniel stopped and looked back at her. "If you would rather earn an honest wage, come by the docks tomorrow morning and ask for a man named Devadas. Tell him Miss Wadeworth sent you. They often need help with odd chores like running errands or carting supplies. He should be able to put you to work."

"Work the Bobbies wouldn't chase me for?" Mouse asked.

"No, it most certainly wouldn't be."

The boy's face brightened. "Yes, Miss. I'll do that. Thank you!" He practically bounced out the door.

Nathaniel smiled at her then followed the boy.

7

TRIXIE looked up when Nathaniel's footsteps echoed on the stairs outside her office.

"I think we need to make that trip to Edinburgh," he suggested as soon as he walked in.

"I was thinking the same thing," she admitted as she stacked the files into a neat pile.

"If I remember correctly it would take about a little over eight hours by train. I'm thinking I should plan on three days to travel there, visit the records room, then travel back to London."

"Just you?" Surely, she misunderstood what he had said. "You plan to leave me here?"

"While I don't like the idea of leaving you here alone I think I can make arrangements for someone to stay with you for protection."

"I would rather go with you."

"No."

The man was exasperating. "Why not?"

"We would be aboard a train with no chaperone for the better part of two days."

"And?" she asked.

"And it wouldn't be proper."

She held her hand up and began ticking off her points. "First, I'm old enough to be considered on-the-shelf. Second, thanks to the scandal attached to Father's disappearance, I'm well beyond the possibility of making a good match."

"I think you're selling yourself short," he interjected.

"No, actually I'm not. I've been told as much by more than one matron."

Nathaniel flinched. "Besides all of that, there's no reason for you to go when I can simply bring you whatever I find."

She glared at him. "Fine, you travel your way. I'll travel mine." She gestured to the air ships just outside her office. "Either way, I'm going."

"You can't be serious."

"Quite." She returned the documents to her lockbox in the drawer and secured both.

"How long would it take to fly one of those things to Edinburgh?"

She crossed her arms over her chest "About half the time of a train."

He growled then paced to the window. "Could you secure a pilot by tomorrow?"

"I can," she said without hesitation.

"Whoever pilots the ship would need to be someone you trust. Someone who won't spread tales of why we made the trip."

"The person I have in mind is quite trustworthy."

She held her breath and waited for him to come to the most logical conclusion, the one where she wasn't left behind. It was her brother who was missing. She wasn't going to just sit by and let someone else handle things. Especially not when she was perfectly capable of searching for him.

"All right," he groused. "What do you need to do to make arrangements?"

She held back her cheer of celebration. "I just need to check the ship register to make sure the one I have in mind is available." She led him downstairs to the office. "Only two of our pilots fly it so it's rarely used." She unlocked the office and led the way to Mrs. Anderson's desk. She lit one of the lamps then retrieved a large tome from its storage place. She scanned the pages until she found the ship she wanted. "As far as I can tell it's free. Mrs. Anderson can confirm that in the morning."

She returned the book to its place and doused the light.

"What about supplies?"

"The ship should be ready to fly. Normally, they are prepared for re-launch as soon as they come in. But again, my dock master can reconfirm that in the morning. I assume you want to make the trip there and back in one day?"

"If that is possible."

"Unless a storm blows in, I think so. I will check with the dock master to see if he's heard of any weather between here and there."

"I want it noted that I do not like this plan very much."

"I didn't expect you too."

When they returned to her office he gathered the files he had brought. "If we are to leave first thing in the morning, we should probably go home." He put his hat on. "I'll escort you."

She gathered her reticule and jacket. "I believe that is a sensible suggestion."

"Glad to know I have them from time to time," he mumbled under his breath making her grin even more.

Out front he hailed a hackney. When they reached her parent's home he helped her down and escorted her to the front door. Her heart fluttered nervously in her chest.

"Shall I pick you up in the morning or would you prefer to meet at Panhurst?"

"Perhaps you should just come to Panhurst. I'm not certain how long it will take me to coordinate everything."

He gave her a brisk nod. "Very well."

"Thank you for seeing me home tonight. And for bringing the files. And well... for everything."

Finally, he smiled. "You're welcome." He took her hand and softly kissed her knuckles.

As before, a shiver of delight ran through her.

"Good night." His voice held just a hint of intimacy.

"Good night."

He waited while she stepped inside. Boldly, she held his gaze as she slowly closed the door. After it latched shut she slumped against the solid wood surface and took a steading breath.

"I don't suppose that grin you're wearing has anything to do with Mr. Dennison, does it?" Mrs. Ellison asked.

"Not directly, no. But Mr. Dennison has agreed to help me find him." She pulled herself away from the door. "Would you mind packing a basket of food for us for tomorrow? We're going to Edinburgh to look for information on Peter's whereabouts."

"To Edinburgh? By one of those air machines, I take it?"

"That's correct."

"I assume I don't have to tell you how improper that is?"

"No, you don't."

Mrs. Ellison harrumphed. "I'll have it ready for you first thing."

"Thank you."

"Is there anything else you'll be needing?"

"Everything else we need will be related to the ship and I'll take care of that in the morning."

"Very good. Just… have a care. I don't want to lose you too."

Trixie hugged Mrs. Ellison. "I will."

~ * ~

The next morning Trixie waited anxiously for Nathaniel to arrive. She had made all the necessary arrangements with Mrs. Anderson and the dock master. Neither of them were fond of her plans, but didn't refuse to help.

As she made her entry in the shipping log, Nathaniel arrived at the port.

"Were you able to secure the ship and a pilot?"

"I have. Everything is ready."

"Which ship will we be taking?" he asked.

She gestured to the *Valkyrie*.

He looked it over then glanced at the ships on either side. "It's quite a bit smaller, isn't it?"

"Yes." Her instinct to defend the *Valkyrie* surfaced. "That means it's lighter, faster, and more nimble."

"Yet, it carries cargo?"

"Not as much as the larger air ships. But Peter designed it to move smaller cargos faster."

He nodded. "And our pilot?"

"The *Valkyrie* is mine," she said with pride. "I'll be piloting her."

"You can't be serious."

His attitude pricked at her temper. "I am quite serious."

He took several steps closer. "I know I said I was worried about your pilot being trustworthy, but I didn't mean for you to go to this extreme."

"This isn't an extreme in my book." She turned on her heel and stomped up the ramp. As expected he followed. "I have been flying since I was fifteen. I learned to fly solo several years ago. I have logged as many hours as half of our pilots." She glared at him. "More than Peter."

"Just because you can fly doesn't mean that you should."

"Give me one good reason why I shouldn't be the one to operate this ship?"

"Because you'll be aboard this ship with an unmarried man and no chaperone for the better part of a day."

She slammed her fists on her hips and faced him. "Are you afraid that I'll ravish you while we're alone?"

He scowled. "No."

She advanced on him. "Are you saying you're not certain you can control your baser instincts and that you're likely to ravish me?"

"Certainly not."

"Do you think that I'll return home and accuse you of improper conduct and demand that you marry me immediately?"

"No."

"Then what is your concern? Because from where I stand, I don't see a rational one."

He growled. "If you were my sister, I would tell her she couldn't do this."

"Well, it's a good thing I'm not your sister."

He gave her an odd look.

She gentled her tone and moved closer. "I understand your concern. Really I do. But please understand that I do not share them. Society turned its back on me at a crucial time in my life. A time when I needed friendship and support, yet there was none to be had. I am beyond giving a damn what those rule makers and followers think."

"I'm sorry you had to deal with your parent's deaths on your own. It shouldn't have been that way." He touched her cheek. "I should have been there for you."

The last of her irritation evaporated. She covered his hand with her own and gave him a sad smile. "You were chasing your own dream. You didn't know what was happening."

"I was running. It just happened to be in the direction of a dream."

"Well, it still worked out for you."

He motioned to the deck of the ship. "Perhaps for you too, in a strange way."

She shrugged. "Perhaps."

He withdrew his hand. "What can I do to help ready the ship?"

Relieved he was going to be reasonable about their trip she said, "First, you need to stow anything you brought with you down there." She pointed to a storage cabinet in the center of the cabin. "Then you can help me check all the lines."

As soon as he added his bag to the cabinet, she showed him how to check the lines. They each took a corner and worked their way around. Thankfully, they found nothing amiss. Not that she expected to. Her dock master ran a tight ship — literally— and checked everything himself. As soon as she was satisfied everything was as it should be, she gave the dock hands the signal to say they were ready for departure. While they waited she showed Nathaniel which ropes he needed to loosen for launch. A few minutes later they received the signal that they were cleared to leave the dock.

She wished she could watch his face as they rose higher in

the air, but there were too many other things to monitor during launch. She'd have to satisfy herself with questioning him later. With Nathaniel watching their tail, she navigated them out of the port and out of the city as if she had been doing it her whole life. Once she adjusted their altitude she motioned him forward.

"What did you think of your first take-off?"

"Breathtaking." He regarded her with a new look in his eye. Perhaps a new level of respect? "I may not know much about flying ships but you seemed to have executed that perfectly."

Her cheeks grew warm at his praise. "I had a good teacher."

"Peter?"

"No, actually, Father taught me the basics, but after he disappeared one of our senior pilots felt sorry for me and let me fly with him. It helped to have something to focus on something other than my grief."

"Do you still fly with him?"

"No. He retired a few months ago." Her eyes twinkled. "There have been a few bets made around the docks about how long he'll stay retired. The larger wagers are split evenly between his wife getting tired of him being underfoot and him getting bored."

Nathaniel chuckled as he leaned against the center cabinets next to where she managed the helm. "You said your brother designed this model?"

"He did."

"We've established it's faster than the train. Which is faster than horseback or carriage. But how does it compare to other airships?"

"He matched it against a couple of our own ships and it came out ahead every time. But like the larger ships, its speed is impacted by the weight of the cargo it carries."

"You mentioned it was meant for smaller loads."

She nodded.

"So why hasn't this become widely known?"

"It is a relatively new model. We've been keeping it somewhat quiet. Only a couple of our established customers have been told of it. However, word is spreading. Peter had been in the process of obtaining financial backing to expand the fleet when he disappeared. The bankers showed up yesterday and made it quite clear that my signature on the documents will not do. I've been holding them off saying he's out of the country on business, but I'm afraid we're going to lose them if I can't find Peter soon and bring him home."

"We'll find him."

8

ABOUT half way through their journey Trixie offered to lock the controls in place so they could break into the picnic basket Mrs. Ellison had packed.

He spread the blanket he had found in one of the cabinets on the deck and coaxed her to come and enjoy the moment with him. They stood at the railing and watched the passing landscape.

"The views are spectacular from here," he told her. "I can see why you like to fly."

"It is peaceful up here. I guess because it's just me and the occasional bird."

He faced her. "I should think you would get lonely."

She shrugged. "Sometimes. But I'm able to see things, do things, and go places very few people have a chance to. And I'm out of reach of the ton and their rules and harsh opinions. It not a bad trade off if you think about it."

They fell silent until he spotted an odd shaped gray mass off to his left. "That's a strange cloud. Do you think it's a storm blowing in?"

A V creased her brow. "I don't think that's a cloud." She ran to the cabin and returned with a telescope. She held it up to her eye and studied the mass.

"What do you think it is?"

Using the scope she handed him, he peered through the long lens. It took a moment to find the strange cloud but when he did nearly dropped the glass. "Is that…" He blinked to clear his vision. "Is that a flock of birds?"

"That's what I thought."

"Birds don't usually fly like that."

"None that I know of."

He handed the glass back to her so she could look again.

"We need to get inside. Now."

He glanced at the mass but followed her into the cabin. "Why? What wrong?"

"I think they're automata."

The gray cloud had flattened out and now appeared to be as wide as the ship.

"You mean like yours?" He pointed to Squeaks and Wings where they had perched on the Captain's post near the navigational controls.

"Do you have a better explanation?"

He grabbed the glass and looked again. The mass had gotten close enough that he could make out smaller individual shapes.

Trixie flipped a few levers, then turned the steering wheel and altered their course away from the mass.

"If they are automata, what do you think the odds are that they will be friendly?" he asked.

She shook her head. "I have no idea what to think right now."

They watched through the window as the mass came closer.

"Your father knew how to build those, right?"

"Yes." She glanced his way. "Do you think they are some of father's creations?"

"I think it's possible. Would you be able to tell by examining them?"

She grimaced. "Maybe. I could tell you if they resembled my mechanicals. Peter would know whether or not they were Father's designs."

"Perhaps we should let them catch up to us," Nathaniel suggested.

"And if they attack us?"

"What's the worst they could do?" he asked.

"Puncture the balloon. In which case we would be lucky to land safely."

"This is your ship. What do you want to do?"

Her eyes darted from the quickly approaching mass to the horizon and back again. "If it were only one or two, I'd say let them approach. It's the fact that there are almost a dozen." She shook her head. "I don't want to think about what they could do together."

"I don't either. Can you outrun them?"

"Maybe." She pointed to a metal handle sticking out of the center console. "Flip that lever there."

He did as she asked without a second thought.

He headed for the cabin door as a flame flickered to life inside the console. He ran to the ship railing in the area closest to the mass. A couple of the automata had gotten closer than he liked.

Their ship picked up speed but it wasn't fast enough to get away from those in the front.

Two of the bird-like mechanical dove toward one of the lines running from the balloon to the deck.

Nathaniel pulled his pistol out and fired at them. One bird jerked to one side, hitting the other, then spiraled downward. The other mechanical bird righted itself and zoomed toward them again.

Nathaniel fired another shot but missed this time.

Trixie shouted from one of the now opened windows of the cabin, "Don't hit the balloon!"

The bird landed on one of the ropes and began to peck at the threads.

Nathaniel grabbed a pole he found hooked along one side of the railing and rushed back to the where the bird had landed. The pole was just long enough that he was able to swat the bird away from the rope. It didn't look as if he'd done any real damage to the bird but it was enough to make it stop pecking at the ropes.

He dropped the pole and reloaded his pistol. When the bird zoomed in again he fired. This time his shot was true. That bird shuddered, then dropped backwards before beginning its spiral descent.

"Hang on," Trixie shouted from her place at the wheel inside the cabin.

He pocketed his pistol and grabbed the closest set of ropes. The ship tipped as she altered their course. Nathaniel had to work to stay on his feet.

He kept one eye on the gray mass behind them and waited for the ship to level out again. The wind picked up as their speed increased. As soon as he could keep his feet beneath him he hurried into the cabin and slammed the door closed behind him.

"Are you all right?" she asked.

"Yes." He allowed himself a moment to catch his breath. "If your father is alive, why would he send mechanicals after you?"

"I think it's more likely that someone took my father's research and created their own version of the automata. At this point, I'm wondering if someone isn't trying to wipe out any evidence that my father was the original creator."

He grimaced. That same thought had already crossed his mind. He just hadn't verbalized it for fear of causing her unnecessary worry.

"I wish we had a way of getting our hands on just one of them," she mumbled.

"We might have the opportunity."

She raised one brow in question.

"It's likely that we will run into them on the way home," he said with false cheer.

She gave him an odd look. "Wonderful."

When they finally pulled far enough ahead of the mass, Nathaniel relaxed his stance and moved away from his post at the rear window. He moved his pistol from his pocket to its holster and joined Trixie at the wheel. "How long can you maintain this speed?"

She checked one of the gauges. "Not much longer."

"I don't see those mechanical birds any more but that

doesn't mean they aren't still out there somewhere."

"I altered our course a couple of times in case they know our destination."

"Is it possible for them to know something like that?"

She shrugged. "Maybe." She gestured to her mechanical pets. "Mine are able to reason though basic concepts like turning left versus right to get to an object. I'm convinced they have learned and stored new information over the years."

"Amazing," he murmured.

9

THEY arrived at the Edinburgh port without further incident. Although the peaceful calm they enjoyed for the first part of their flight never returned. They both remained on alert, constantly scanning the sky for threats. Yet, she still enjoyed Nathaniel's company.

He demonstrated that he wasn't afraid to get his hands dirty by helping her ready the ship for landing. Somehow he'd avoided picking up the snobby behavior his mother, and even occasionally his eldest brother, displayed. Just because the Dennison family held a Viscount's title didn't make them better than anyone else. At least not in her book.

Nathaniel watched everything. And, unless she were mistaken, he enjoyed himself immensely. Once they docked and the lines had been secured, he followed her down the ramp.

"I'm going to dash over to the port office and fill out the arrival documents. You'll wait here?" she asked.

He scanned the bustling piers around them. "Are you sure you don't want me to come with you?"

"If you are planning to visit the local RIO, I believe you would be better off spending a few minutes cleaning up." She ran one finger down his cheek then showed him the soot covered tip.

He looked down at his hands and shirt then grimaced. "You're probably right."

"I'm afraid that happens when you pass through the haze

that hovers over most of the larger cities." She gestured to the cabin. "There's a mirror inside one of the cabinet doors directly behind the wheel. There should also be a container of water and clean towels."

"I don't like the idea of you wandering about the port without me. There are more people here than I care for."

"It's always crowded this time of day." She patted his chest. "I've filled out many port documents. I promise it will only take a few moments."

He frowned. "Which building is it?"

She tipped her head in the direction of the busiest building. "Just there."

"The one with all of the notices posted along the front wall."

"That's the one."

"Very well. At least take a couple of your automata with you."

She held open the pocket of her skirt. "As if I could leave them."

"All right. Just hurry."

"I will." For a moment she thought he might kiss her. But that would be highly improper in a crowded area. Still, she practically skipped down the ramp in her giddiness. Just before she merged into the congestion of people on the pier she glanced back. Sure enough, he was watching her.

How long had it been since someone other than Mrs. Ellison worried about her well-being? Peter cared about her but he treated her as more of a peer than a sister. Not that she would tolerate any handholding or pampering from him.

As expected, the paperwork only took a moment to complete. It was always the same three questions about where they came from, what goods were they bringing in, and when they expected to depart.

When she finished she pushed her way back through the crowd to the *Valkyrie*.

She glanced through one of the cabin windows before opening the door to make sure it was safe. In the short time she'd been gone Nathaniel had managed to wash up, don a clean shirt, and slip his jacket on. From the expression on his face she could tell his investigator persona had been restored. Part of her was disappointed. The other part was intrigued. After all, his serious "I'm working" side was, well… appealing.

"That didn't take long," she remarked as she entered the cabin.

He tugged on his sleeve as he faced her. "I'm afraid your towel is worse for the wear now though."

She shrugged one shoulder. "That's what it's there for."

"Everything go all right with the port office?"

She went to the cabinet to gather her things. "Of course."

"What did you tell them was the reason for our visit?"

She waved her hand to dismiss the question. "I told them I had a shipment to pick up."

"That's it?"

"That's it." She pulled her reticule from one of the compartments then went to the cabinet that held the mirror and washbasin. "Do you mind if I take a moment to clean up also?"

"No. Go right ahead." He gathered his hat and cane. "Would you like for me to wait outside for you?"

"Not necessary."

He blinked in surprise.

"I don't plan to change clothes, only wash the soot off."

He drew close and touched the tip of her nose.

"But you wear it well, my dear." He winked then added, "I'll wait right outside anyway." With a flip of his wrist his hat landed squarely on his head. The roar of the crowded pier flowed in when he opened the cabin door. He stepped outside and closed her in once again.

Using one of the clean towels she washed her face and hands then neatened her hair. She gave her blouse and skirts a quick inspection and decided they would be passable for strolling about town. Her skirt had enough material to pass for a walking dress even though it was actually a split riding skirt. Normally she would have worn trousers to captain the ship but her worry that Nathaniel would have been scandalized had won out.

In truth, she had probably not given him enough credit. After all, his mother's behavior didn't necessarily reflect his thoughts.

She pinned her hat in place then slipped into her own jacket.

"Come along Squeaks. Nid, you too." She held her reticule open for her pets to climb in. "Wings, you and Hopper keep an eye on *Valkyrie* for me."

Wings spread her wings and bobbed at her in acknowledgement.

She opened one of the upper cabin windows so her pets could slip in and out if they needed. "I should think we'll be back before dinner."

She joined Nathaniel on deck and locked the cabin door behind her.

"Are you ready?" he asked.

"I believe so." She took his offered arm.

"Will the *Valkyrie* will be safe?"

She nodded. "Yes. We have an agreement with some of the dock personnel. They keep an eye on all Panhurst ships that come in to make sure they aren't tampered with and to minimize stowaways."

"How reliable are they?"

"Well, we don't expect them to act as security only report to the captain if anyone suspicious has been near the ships. More of an alert that we need to check and re-check before departing."

"Ah."

"The dock workers don't want the ships tampered with any more than the captains or owners. It's too dangerous. One explosion or collision in the port could set off a chain reaction that any of them could be caught in."

"I hadn't thought of it in that way. That actually relieves my mind."

She patted his arm. "So where are we headed today?"

At the entrance to the port he waved down a hackney.

"To Queens Street. I had thought we could do a bit of shopping."

She frowned at him. "You must be joking."

"Not at all."

When the hackney came to a stop, he negotiated with the driver then helped her up. She waited until he was settled then pinned him with her stare. "Shopping? I know we didn't come to Edinburgh to go shopping. What are you up to?"

"Nothing at all," he said with false enthusiasm.

Squeaks scampered out of her bag and ran across the seat. She climbed onto Nathaniel's leg and watched him.

Trixie snorted. "Apparently Squeaks has taken a liking to you."

"She has good taste."

"I'm beginning to question that," she mumbled.

He leaned closer. "I need for you to trust me for a little while. Can you do that?"

She gazed into his eyes. She didn't need to think about it. She trusted him. Far more than she should. After all what did she really know about Nathaniel? Most of her knowledge came from memories or things she'd heard from other people. Yet her heart and her instincts said she could depend on this man. That he was there to help her and he would protect her if he could.

"Yes. I can do that."

He reached for her hand and gave it a gentle squeeze.

"That doesn't mean I have to like being kept in the dark," she added.

He chuckled. "I wouldn't expect you to."

While he was distracted, Squeaks dashed into his jacket pocket. Trixie smiled, but didn't mention anything about him having a passenger.

When they arrived at their destination, Nathaniel exited then helped her down. He paid the driver then offered his arm to her. They strolled along the bustling sidewalk as if they were simply enjoying an afternoon out. Finally he stopped in front of a milliner's window.

She raised a brow in question. "Needing something for a lady friend?"

"Hardly. Do you see that building just there?"

He pointed to the image reflected in the storefront glass.

"Yes."

"The one I need to go in is just on the other side of it. I won't get away with taking an escort of any kind inside so I thought you might spend an hour or two shopping. My treat."

"You're offering to pacify me with gifts? How very bourgeoisie of you."

"Consider it a healthy alternative to breaking and entering."

She harrumphed. "Anything in particular I should buy while I'm here?"

"Whatever your little heart desires." He slipped a handful of notes into her reticule.

"I could use a new wrap." She tapped the side of her jaw. "Perhaps something in black?"

"Pink would be far more appealing on you." He raised her hand to his lips but instead of kissing the top he turned her hand over and he pressed his lips to inside of her wrist.

Trixie's heart flip-flopped in her chest and her lips parted on a gasp.

His lips twitched. "Stay out of trouble. I'll meet you shortly."

She stood shock still as he hurried across the street. She rubbed her wrist where it still tingled from his touch. When she looked up he had blended into the crowd and she couldn't easily pick him out.

Oooooh. He was a devil.

And he knew exactly how to distract her.

10

THE Edinburgh intelligence office was hidden beneath a seemingly innocuous space. If observed for any time, one might think the building housed a gentleman's club or perhaps a series of bachelor apartments despite the accounting firm occupying one end. Knowing a direct and honest approach would work best, Nathaniel accessed the RIO through the middle entrance.

An older scholarly gentleman looked up from his desk in the foyer. "May I help you, sir?"

"Good morning. I do hope I'm in the right place. My friend, Mr. Glastone, told me I might locate a few of my colleges here." Nathaniel touched the pin he wore on his lapel that signified him as a Royal Intelligence Officer.

"It's very likely sir. Your name is?"

"Nathaniel Dennison."

"And what brings you to our fair city, Mr. Dennison?"

"I'm in the process of developing a business proposal, but need a little help with some of the details. I had hoped some of my Edinburgh colleagues might have some information that will point me in the right direction."

The man left his pen in the crease of his book and stood. "Perhaps I can help you find some of your colleagues, Mr. Dennison." He waved Nathaniel toward the door at the end of foyer. "Right this way." The man pulled a key from his waistcoat and unlocked the door. He knocked twice, paused, then once again. The sound of a bolt sliding to one side echoed through the heavy wood then the handle turned and the door opened. On the other side lay a narrow hallway. The walls and ceiling were lined with dark wood panels. A guard stood at attention by the door. The man said to the guard, "Alexander, this is Mr. Dennison from the London office. I'm going to escort him to the records room. I should only be a moment."

The guard said nothing. He didn't even twitch in acknowledgement.

Nathaniel's escort pressed a hidden notch in one of the panels, opening a second door. This door led to a large, brightly lit sitting room. The dark wood and masculine setting were typical of any gentleman's club. There were small groupings of chairs scattered about the room. Some were paired with a table or free-standing ash tray. At this hour it was no surprise to find only a couple of people in attendance.

He followed his escort through two more doors, down two sets of stairs and a long hallway. By his estimation, they were beneath the street he had crossed when he left Trixie.

"How long have you been with the organization?" Nathaniel asked.

"Twenty three years. And you, sir?"

"Five."

The man glanced at his pin. "And already a senior investigator?"

Nathaniel shrugged. "I have a knack for puzzles."

"Hmmmm."

They turned left at the end of the passage way and the man used his key to open yet another heavy wood door. "George, this is Mr. Dennison from the London office."

The man working at the desk spun his wheelchair and faced them.

Nathaniel's original escort continued. "He is working on a case and would like access to our records. Would you be so kind as to assist him?"

"Delighted," George remarked.

"I will leave you in George's capable hands so I can return to my desk out front," Nathaniel's escort said.

"Thank you."

"So what can I help you find, Mr. Dennison?" George asked.

"I need everything you have on scientists or inventors who have disappeared in the last ten years, whether we conducted a full investigation or not."

"Hmmm." George furrowed his brow. "I believe Mr. Morris looked into something along those lines about two years ago."

"Did he find anything of interest?"

"Wouldn't know. He never had a chance to finish it. He died in a carriage accident."

"What happened to his case files?"

"They were packed up by his superior. Any open cases would have been reassigned."

"Do you know who would have taken that case?"

"Don't know that there was an official case made of it. As I recall he was following a lead to see where it might go." He shrugged. "You know how those go. Some pan out, others not."

Nathaniel nodded. "I do. Don't suppose his notes were kept?"

"They were indeed." George wheeled himself to the wall lined with drawers. "I like to keep a file on each of our officers." He rummaged in one of the drawers then pulled out a packet of documents and notebooks. "Here we are." George pointed to a cleared off place in the middle of a row of shelves. "This is everything that wasn't part of an active case."

Nathaniel flipped through the pages of handwritten notes. Some had been made to resemble entries in a journal. Others appeared to be random thoughts. Almost all of the recent notes mentioning missing persons had a short series of numbers and letters scribbled above them.

"George, do you have any idea what this is?"

Nathaniel pointed to the strange notation when George wheeled himself over and peered at the page. "That is probably one of our dead case numbers."

"Can you show me where to find it?"

"That will be in the back." George led the way deeper into the file room where row after row of boxed files were stored. "Ah. Here we are." George pulled one of the boxes forward on the shelf. It was the only one in that area without a layer of dust.

"I'm guessing Mr. Morris returned to this box more than once?"

"Yes, actually."

"May I?" Nathaniel gestured to the box.

George scooted back to give Nathaniel room. "Go right ahead. Any idea what you're looking for?"

"Not immediately, no. Still trying to determine what Mr. Morris' line of thinking was with his notes."

"May have been nothing."

"Maybe. However, I like to be thorough." Nathaniel opened the box and revealed multiple files. Each one had been labeled with a different name. Perhaps a series of missing people?

"You're welcome to move the box to the table where you were working."

"I will if I feel I need to dig into it deeper. Mostly, I just want to see if there is any commonality in the files."

"Ah. Well, I'll leave you to it then."

Nathaniel murmured this thanks as he dug into the files. As soon as George scooted away, Trixie's mechanical mouse climbed out of his pocket. The tiny mechanical ran down his sleeve and onto the edge of the box. He too peered down into the contents. "What are you doing here?" he whispered.

Nathaniel shook off the notion that the mouse might answer and continued digging through the box. The files had been labeled with names. Some he recognized but couldn't place where he knew them. He made notes in his book of those that stood out. Trixie's pet leapt forward and sniffed the air around one of the folders. When it disappeared between the tabs of one Nathaniel pulled it up to review.

Thomas Alexander Wadeworth. Trixie's father?

Nathaniel opened the folder wider and scanned the documents. He found a report on her father's disappearance, including information about the wreckage. There were enough details about the wreckage that Nathaniel wondered if it had been fully investigated. And if so, why had it not been assigned a case number?

Trixie's pet tugged on his sleeve. When he glanced down, the creature ran deeper into the pile of documents.

Nathaniel went back to reading the report.

Trixie's pet once again tugged on his sleeve then ran down into the folder.

He didn't have time to play games. He needed to finishing reading then get back to Trixie. He dug along the side of the box feeling for the mischievous little imp. Instead, of the mechanical toy he found something square and flat lying flat on the bottom, beneath the standing folders.

He carefully worked it out from under the folders. It was a book of some kind. It had several scratches and had been smudged with soot. Despite its somewhat abused condition, the lock remained intact. The monogram on the spine read "TAW". Thomas Alexander Wadeworth. Was this the journal Trixie needed?

The mechanical mouse glanced at the book then up at him expectantly. "All right," he whispered then slipped the book into his jacket pocket. As he finished flipping through the files his new little friend climbed back into his pocket. Nathaniel noted a few more names then returned the lid and pushed the box back into place.

He checked Mr. Morris' notes one more time to ensure he'd missed nothing. When he could glean nothing else, he returned the documents to the file and collected his hat and cane.

"Would you like me to return Mr. Morris' file to its place?" Nathaniel asked as he approached George's desk.

"Not necessary. I'll take care of it," George assured him.

Nathaniel handed the file over.

"Did you find what you needed?" George asked.

"I'm not certain. I made note of a few things to follow up

on when I return to London." Nathaniel extended his hand. "I appreciate your assistance, George."

"You're very welcome. And good luck with your investigation, sir."

"I assume I return the way I came in?"

"Yes." George wheeled himself to the door, unlocked the multiple locks, then touched a button to open the door. By Nathaniel's estimations, the trigger was likely the only thing that enabled George to manage the heavy door. "Any of the guards can show you the way if you if you get turned around though."

"Very good." Nathaniel tipped his head. "Good day."

"Good day to you, sir."

Nathaniel retraced his steps back to the lounge. As soon as he crossed the threshold, someone called out his name. He scanned the room for the source. An older gentlemen sitting near the fireplace caught his eye. Without saying a word, the gentleman invited him over.

"I understand you're one of Glastone's men," the man said when Nathaniel approached.

Something about the man's presence commanded his attention. "Yes, sir, I am."

The man gestured to the chair across from him. "Your name?"

"Dennison, sir. Nathaniel Dennison." He extended his hand to the man.

The man shook, but didn't release him immediately. He squinted up at him. "One of James Dennison's boys?"

"The youngest."

"Ah." He released his hold on Nathaniel's hand. "Your older brother now holds the title, correct."

"Yes, sir."

"How is he handling it?"

Nathaniel shrugged as he took his seat. "William was born into the role. Father had ample time to prepare him before he passed, so I believe he will do well."

The man grunted his agreement.

"Forgive me, sir, but you are?" Nathaniel raised his brow in question.

"Richardson. Colonel Richardson."

Nathaniel barely restrained the impulse to snap to attention.

"I assume you've heard of me, then?" the older man said with a lift of his brow.

"Yes, sir, I have. Your efforts in the Sardinian coup are still whispered about with a touch of awe."

The Colonel snorted. "Likely an exaggeration."

Nathaniel shrugged. "Even so, I'm pleased to finally meet you."

"I've been hearing positive things about you, Mr. Dennison. What brings you to our neighborhood?"

"I'm following a lead related to the Mastermind."

"Did they finally put you on that case?"

"All of us work it when we can. But I am intrigued by the many unknowns."

"And it led you to Edinburgh?"

"Not directly, no. I came to see what information your investigators had on what I believe to be peripheral cases."

"And what did you find?"

Nathaniel smiled. "More cases to review."

"Seems to be the way of it, doesn't it? Dammed frustrating. Whoever this mastermind is has a knack for sending us in circles. Every time we get close, the trail goes cold."

"We'll find him."

"Yes, but will we all be cold in our grave by then?"

"I for one, hope not," Nathaniel said sincerely.

"Well perhaps you will have more luck than the rest of us, young man."

"I don't believe in luck, sir."

A man approached and whispered in the Colonel's ear. The Colonel nodded then looked at Nathaniel. "I'm sorry to cut this short but there is something I must attend to."

Nathaniel got to his feet when the Colonel did. "It was a pleasure to meet you, Mr. Dennison. Henry can show you the way out if you've finished your business here."

"I have." He shook the Colonel's hand. "Thank you, sir."

"Give Glastone my regards."

"I shall." He watched the man who, if you believed the stories, single-handedly saved the crown twice by intercepting and decoding assassination attempts and returning false information to the enemy. Perhaps one day his service would be as equally valuable.

In the meantime, he had a lunch date to keep.

11

TRIXIE slammed the book she had been reading closed with a little more force than she'd intended.

Why was it taking Nathaniel so long? Had he been arrested for going someplace he shouldn't have? He acted as if he would be allowed to enter the local intelligence office. What if he had been wrong?

She wasn't certain how much time had passed since he left but it had to have been several hours. After all, she'd explored five different boutiques, a bookstore, and now she'd consumed most of a pot of tea. Even the lure of her new book couldn't distract her from worrying about Nathaniel and whether something had happened to him.

She absently drummed her finger on the table as she stared out the window. What were her options for action?

Naturally, she could choose to wait indefinitely for him. Waiting only made her anxious. She could give up, return to her airship, and forget the entire plan. Her stomach turned just thinking about leaving Nathaniel without knowing what happened to him much less if he had found anything about father or Peter's disappearance. She could march up to the door of the building Nathaniel had described and demand to be let in. She grimaced. That would only call attention to herself and invite trouble.

"Have you been waiting long?"

Trixie startled at the question. She quelled her impulse to launch herself into Nathaniel's arms and demand he never leave her behind like that again. "Of course not." With a heavy dose of false calm, she gestured to the empty seat across from her. "Tea?"

"Please. And biscuits too, if you don't mind."

"Not at all." She signaled for the waitress. As soon as the young lady left to fill their request, she asked him, "Did you learn anything?"

"Afraid not."

She blinked, uncomprehending. Surely he jested. "Well—"

"How was your shopping?"

"Boring, actually."

"I'm sorry to hear that."

She started to question him more but her cut her off.

"Did you try the bookseller on the corner?"

"Of course. It was the most interesting place on the block."

"Is that a new book then?" He pointed to the one she had left on the table.

"Yes, it is. Are you sure you didn't learn anything?"

"Quite. What is your new book about?" His abrupt dismissal of her question made her grit her teeth.

"It's a novel about an inspector and his colleague who are hunting for a missing mummy. If you didn't learn anything then what took you so long?"

"Just chatting with some of the men in the club." He pointed to her book. "It looks as if you've started reading it. Do you like the book so far?"

She narrowed her gaze at him. Why was he acting so strange? Perhaps he didn't want to share what he found out. "No, actually, I'm not enjoying the book. I've been quite disappointed in the inspector. He's been behaving quite oddly."

"That's a shame. Perhaps it will be better later on. You shouldn't give up on a book after only a few chapters."

"Hmmm." She stared at him and tried to figure out what was going on in his head.

The waitress returned with the things they had requested. As soon as she left again, Nathaniel began a long diatribe about the benefits of tea on the body. Despite consuming several biscuits and two cups of tea, he somehow managed to keep up his monologue and effectively blocked her every time she started to ask a question.

Had they been in a less public place she would have given him an earful. Instead, she forced a smile and silently prayed he would choke on a bite so she could get a word in.

He paid for their food and once again offered her his arm. She debated refusing it but finally relented. When they reached the end of the block he leaned closer. "We're being watched. Ask no questions about your father. I'll share what I learned when we return to the ship."

She stiffened her spine. They were being watched? By whom?

She assumed the role of chatty companion and told him in excruciating detail every one of the scarves she found in the boutiques until Nathaniel hailed a hackney for their return to port. He handed her up into the carriage then waited for a sign from him that it was safe.

Once they set off he took her hand into his and began to draw on her palm with his finger. It took a moment but she quickly realized he was drawing letters trying to tell her something.

N-O-T-S-A-F-E.

She nodded she understood and remained silent for the rest of their ride.

They exited the carriage in a new part of town instead of the port.

"Come, dear." Nathaniel held his hand out to help her down. "Perhaps we'll be able to find that scarf you wanted here."

Playing along with his charade, she batted her eyes at him. "But I thought you said I'd spent my allowance already?"

"Consider it my way of making up to you after leaving you alone for so long while I chatted with my friends."

She took his arm. "I'm afraid it may take more than a scarf to accomplish that, dear."

"Now, now."

In her ear he whispered, "We'll duck into a shop and try to find a way out the back."

She nodded once to let him know she'd heard. He led her into one of the larger shops and paid one of the workers to show them another way out.

When they stepped into the back alley, he pulled her quickly to the end, then around the corner and into another shop. There he pulled her into a darkened corner and gestured for her to riffle through whatever was on the table. Finally he tugged on her elbow and urged her to leave. They went the other direction on the street and boarded a hackney they found waiting at the corner. This one he directed to the port.

"I believe we lost them but I won't know for certain until we reach the port," he told her in a low tone.

"Who was following us?"

"I'm not certain." He took her hand in his. "How long will it take you to ready the ship to leave?"

"Not long. I left an order to have fuel delivered to the dock. It should be waiting when we return. It would only be a matter of getting permission and a departure time from the port master. My size ship usually doesn't take long."

He nodded. "Try to secure one for as quickly as possible."

"To return to London?"

"Must you declare your return location for departure?"

"Yes." She shrugged. "But I can always correct my records in London to show what I want."

"Good. I am not sure I want to return directly to London with this." He pulled a book from his coat pocket and handed it to her.

She gasped. "You found Father's journal."

12

TRIXIE traced the edge of the outline of the metal heart that enclosed the lock mechanism with the tip of her finger. "I never expected to see Father's journal again." Tears had pooled in her eyes when she looked up. "Where did you find it?"

"In the records room." He pulled the mechanical mouse from his pocket and let it run from his palm to hers. "Actually, your little friend is the one that found it."

She touched the metal mouse on the nose. "How do you suppose Father's journal come to be in the records room?"

He shook his head. "I don't know." He peered out the window of the carriage. "I'm afraid I have more questions than answers in this and I don't like it very much."

"You'll work it out." She squeezed his hand.

He looked at her. "It is good being with you again, Trixie."

She put her free hand on his forearm. "You, too."

For a moment he considered kissing her. In the privacy of the carriage, no would even notice. But if he did, he might not want to stop and right now he needed all of his wits to keep them safe. Whoever had been following them was likely not a friend to them. He wasn't about to risk Trixie's safety just to satisfy his craving.

Instead he changed the subject. "I presume you can land your airship in just about any open field."

"I can. Why?"

"I know someplace we can go instead of London."

"Where?"

"A friend of mine owns an estate not far from here. He would be in a position to help if trouble did follow."

"Will you be putting others in danger, do you think?"

"I won't know until we set off." He shrugged. "Even if we are followed, Carrick won't mind. He's always spoiling for a good fight."

"I see."

The hackney stopped near the port entrance. Nathaniel scanned the area for threats as he paid the driver. When he didn't see anything out of the ordinary he helped Trixie step down.

As they entered the still-bustling port she asked in a low tone, "What do you want me to do?"

"Just act as you normally would. Get whatever permissions you need to from the port, but avoid saying more than you have to. Once we're in the air I'll direct you."

She tipped her head in acknowledgement.

They hurried to her ship. He carried the fuel that had been delivered aboard. Once everything had been safely stored she ran to get permission to depart. He hated letting her leave his sight for even a moment, but hovering over her would be abnormal. Besides, he didn't want to risk anyone sneaking board the ship while they were away.

Trixie's mechanical creatures scampered about the deck as he checked the lines the way she had shown him. He kept one eye on the port building and didn't relax until he spotted Trixie again.

"Everything all right?" she asked when she stepped onto the deck of the ship.

"It is now. Did they say when we could depart?"

"Yes. We have permission to leave as soon as we're ready."

"That seems rather easy."

"My ship moves quickly and doesn't need port assistance. Their only requirement is that we depart well before the Endeavor at quarter past three."

"Shall we set off then?"

"Yes. Let me make one last check of the lines."

She danced from one line to the other, pulling and tugging on the ropes and retying knots where needed. Finally she returned and declared, "All right, let's be off."

He smiled down at her. "What can I do to help?"

"Same as before. Watch the tail as we exit and let me know if we veer too close to anything."

"I can do that." He opened the windows facing the rear of the ship so she could hear him yell from the deck.

"What direction should I take?" she asked.

"Head for London until I tell you otherwise."

"All right."

Like their London departure, she maneuvered the craft without incident. As soon as they cleared the port he returned to the cabin. From there he alternated watching the sky behind them and the landmarks below.

Trixie had spread a map across the desk next to the captain's post. Her mechanicals kept it in place.

"This is Carrick's land." He circled a spot on the map with his finger. "There's a large open field west of the carriage house where you should be able to land. If that won't work, the one to the south is another option. We would just have a longer hike to the main house."

"As long as the area is reasonably flat with no trees to snag the lines or puncture the body we will be fine."

"Can you land in the dark?"

"It's not my preference but if I have to, yes."

"We should make it well before dusk, but I wanted to make sure you'd be comfortable just in case."

They rode in silence for several moments before she said, "Thank you for bringing me Father's journal."

"You're welcome." He glanced her way. "I'm just sorry you won't be able to read it."

She frowned in confusion. "Why can't I?"

"Based on the scratches around the lock mechanism I'm guessing one of the RIO investigators tried to break open the lock and failed. More than once. Not to be rude, but if they couldn't break the lock I doubt you will be successful either."

"I don't need to break the lock. I have the key."

It was his turn to be surprised. "Oh. Well, good. Then I hope it brings back many happy memories of your family."

"Oh, it's not a journal like you would think. Father recorded his experiments and calculations in this."

"You mean for his inventions and things?"

"Yes."

Another piece fell into place in Nathaniel's mind. "Wouldn't your father have kept something like that hidden away?"

"Only for formal occasions or when Mother insisted. Normally, he kept it with him at all times."

"You said you thought he had it with him when his ship crashed, correct?"

"Yes, he would have. That's why I'm curious how someone here obtained it."

"Me too," he muttered. "May I inspect the book while you are busy?"

"Of course." She handed him the book.

He inspected the outer casing. It was made of some type of metal. He tipped it toward the sunlight. It was far too sturdy to be tarnished silver as he originally thought. The material was surprisingly lightweight yet durable. There were multiple cogs and wheels layered across the cover within a heart shaped base. Scorch marks indicated the book had been exposed to high heat and, as he'd already pointed out, scratches around the hinges and lock mechanism hinted someone had tried to force their way in. Yet all of the pieces remained intact.

Like the woman flying the *Valkyrie* and the creatures running about the desk, the book was a marvel.

13

NATHANIEL pointed out a field not far from a manor house. A dense treed area surrounded the property with large open fields on either side. Even from their height she could tell the estate was an older one. The largest building resembled a fortress. It reminded her of the ruins of a Norman castle she'd seen on holiday.

"Your friend lives here?" she asked.

"Most of the year. He does keep a house in London for the times he needs to conduct business or social obligations. But he prefers the country."

"What if he's not in residence?"

"Then Gerard will make us welcome in his stead."

"Gerard?"

"Carrick's brother."

"You're certain they won't mind us dropping in unannounced?"

"Quite."

Trixie maneuvered the ship around so it faced the direction she preferred for takeoff. As they made the final descent, she tasked Nathaniel with manning the lines and watching the tail.

Taking off and landing in the country was far more pleasant than the city. The air was clear and fresh unlike the sooty, grimy fog that hovered over most large cities. Most people living and working in the city didn't notice what they were forced to breathe, but once you rose above the dinginess of it all the difference was remarkable.

They had just set the ship down on firm ground when one of her pets scurried up her arm and clamored for her attention. Wings flapped about and drew her attention to the group of armed men who had spread out between them and the direction of the manor.

"Nathaniel, I do hope those are friends of yours," she said with a tip of her head toward the men.

"Ah, yes. The one in the middle is Carrick." He waved to the men. "Ho, Carrick!"

Two of the men held back while the one he had indicated as Carrick continued toward them along with two other men.

"Nathan." Carrick called out. "What the devil are you doing this way? We thought we were being invaded by a foreign entity."

Nathaniel laughed, then asked Trixie, "Are you situated enough for me to head off Carrick?"

"Yes, go ahead."

He went to greet his friends then led them closer to the ship.

Her shyer pets scattered into the closest hiding hole.

"Beatrix, allow me to present Lord Carrick Malcom Jamison, the third. Carrick, this is Miss Beatrix Wadeworth."

"Pleased to make your acquaintance," Carrick said with a beaming grin. "You must tell us all about this wonderful ship that I understand belongs to you."

Carrick was about the same height as Nathaniel, perhaps a bit taller, but broader through the shoulders. He had light brown hair but the copper strands that caught the sunlight hinted his family might have a few Scottish connections.

She tipped her head to him. "It's lovely to meet you as well. I apologize for dropping in on you like this, Lord Jamison. I hope we haven't damaged anything in your field."

"Oh, absolutely not. Nothing here to worry over. Nathan knows these lands well enough. He directed you to the best spot, I'm sure. And do call me Carrick. All that Lordship nonsense is far too stuffy for me." He gestured to the ship. "Is there anything you need a hand with?"

"If someone could grab each of these ropes—" She pointed to the four ropes attached to each of the corners. "They need to be secured to something sturdy or tethered to the ground with a spike."

Carrick motioned for the two men who had accompanied him to help while he and Nathan took the remaining lines.

"What the devil?" one of the men bellowed.

Trixie head swiveled to see what had startled the man. Wings had flown over to greet the man and currently circled above him.

The other man dropped his rope and pulled his pistol out.

"Wait! Don't hurt her," Trixie yelled. "She just wants to greet you to make sure you aren't a threat."

"What kind of bird is that?" Carrick asked.

"It's a mechanical bird that her father made," Nathaniel told Carrick. "It's quite impressive."

"Wings! Come here at once. You're scaring the poor man," Trixie yelled from the deck.

Wings changed directions and flew to Trixie's outstretched hand.

"That was very naughty," she scolded the bird. "You know you must allow me to introduce you to new people."

The bird hung its head.

Trixie ran her finger across Wings back to let her know she wasn't angry. "Now, let's do this properly." Wings hopped onto the side of Trixie's hand where she could perch prettily. Then Trixie held her hand out toward the men. "Gentlemen, this is Wings. She is one of my mechanical pets. She alerts me when strangers are nearby and has been known to chase off more than one pick pocket."

"You said that is just one of your pets?" one of the men asked.

"Yes. I also brought along Nid, my spider, and Squeaks, the mouse. I also have a mechanical rabbit, squirrel, and scorpion at home."

"Amazing," Carrick said. To Nathaniel he added, "Gerard will love those."

"I don't care for real spiders. Not sure a mechanical would be any better," one of the men said and gave an exaggerated shudder.

"Nid isn't scary." Trixie encouraged Wings to light upon her shoulder then pulled Nid from her pocket. She held him out on her open palm for the men to see. "He's quite calm and he responds well to commands."

"Can he spin webs?" the other man asked as he tentatively touched Nid.

She smiled. "No, thankfully not. I cannot imagine what kind of messes he would make if he could."

"You said you brought a mouse also?" the first man asked.

"Yes. She's hiding somewhere in the cabin." Trixie gestured to the enclosed space. "Actually, I should go and locate her before we go."

"Go ahead, Miss. We'll secure these ropes."

"Thank you." She slipped Nid back into her pocket. As she passed Nathaniel, she paused and quietly asked, "Will we be staying long?"

"Only long enough to get a sense of what we know and to plan our next steps. Perhaps a day or two."

"In that case, I'll close off the burner. No sense in leaving it open if there is no one to watch it."

"Do you need someone to watch over your ship?" Carrick asked.

"Not necessarily. As long as you think no one will venture close enough to take the lines or parts off the burner. So few know how to fly one that I'm not worried about it being taken away."

"I can have the stable boys take turns watching it. They're likely to get a kick out of it anyway."

"That would be wonderful. Thank you," she said.

Once she had done what she could to secure the ship for any weather that might roll in she grabbed the bag she had brought with her personal items. She encouraged both Squeaks and Wings to hide inside the bag so neither of them would be lost on the way to the house.

Nathaniel raised a brow at her bag. "Did you know that we would be gone longer than expected?"

"I always expect the unexpected. I've traveled enough to know it never hurts to have a spare change of clothing and the bare necessities stashed somewhere."

He patted his own satchel. "Agreed."

Carrick ordered one of the men to stay behind with the ship. The others fanned out around them as they set out for the castle.

"So what brings you to my door, Nathan?" Carrick asked. "You're not hiding from your mother again, are you?"

Nathaniel chuckled. "Nothing nearly as sinister as that. We were being followed in Edinburgh while investigating something. I needed someplace safe for Trixie where we could take a moment and review what we know about this case and maybe figure out who is so interested in us."

"Which of you is being followed?" Carrick asked.

"In truth," Nathaniel glanced her way. "I'm not certain."

Trixie stumbled. Peter disappeared. Her father and mother disappeared and were presumed dead. Could it all be related? When Nathaniel had told her they were being followed, she assumed it had something to do with him being in the RIO. It hadn't occurred to her that she might be the reason.

Nathaniel reached for her hand. "We'll figure it out."

"I hope we aren't bringing trouble to your door," she told Carrick.

"I, for one, hope you do," Carrick said. "It's been dreadfully dull around here."

The other two men murmured their agreement. Nathaniel chuckled.

She blinked in surprise. Did all men crave action and adventure, even at the risk of injury or death, or was it only the ones she came in contact with?

When they broke free of the dense cluster of trees she got her first glimpse of the manor from the ground. The flat walls of the towers were as grand as they were intimidating. She could well imagine the building surviving decades of weather and local squirmishes.

They had just set foot on the gravel path when a shot rang out.

Nathaniel knocked her to the ground and used his body to cover her.

"Over there!" one of Carrick's men shouted.

Every time she tried to lift her head to see what was happening Nathaniel stopped her. "Stay down," he whispered in her ear. Her heart pounded against her chest and every instinct she had demanded she run.

Another shot rang out. Based on the proximity of the sound, she guessed that Carrick or one of his men had returned fire. There was yet another gunshot, then footsteps and shouting.

"Move to the hedges," Carrick told them. "We'll cover you."

Nathaniel rolled off her then pulled her to her feet. "Stay low," he ordered as he tugged her toward the row of bushes running along the road. As soon as they reached the greenery he pushed her to the ground. "Don't move unless I or Carrick tell you otherwise."

"All right." Blood pounded in her ears making it hard to hear much over the sound.

Nathaniel sat with his back to the hedges and pulled his pistol from his jacket. He checked the bullets then looked in Carrick's direction.

Carrick had also moved against the hedge but was several carriage lengths away. He peered through the foliage, signaled something to Nathaniel, and then crept forward.

Two more shots rang out then someone shouted, "Clear."

Trixie looked to Nathaniel expectantly. He held up one finger telling her to wait.

Another man yelled, "All clear." Finally a third man repeated the message.

The tension in Nathaniel's frame eased. "I think we're fine, but stay put until Carrick returns."

She nodded her understanding. She was still too shaken to

stand anyway. As they waited, she took a few deep breaths to calm herself. She and Nathaniel were fine. She said a quick prayer that none of Carrick's men had been hurt either.

Someone seemed determined to catch them. She swallowed the lump that had formed in her throat. Or kill them.

The crunching of a twig on the other side of the shrub sent Nathaniel on alert. He aimed his pistol down the line of shrubs. "Ho, Nathaniel. It's just us," Carrick called out.

Nathaniel relaxed his stance and got to his feet.

"I assume your men caught whoever fired that shot?" Nathaniel ask as he reached to help Trixie stand.

"They did. Unfortunately, the poor bloke they found won't be answering any questions."

"Damn," Nathaniel muttered.

"Any idea who it is?" Trixie asked as she brushed the grass and leaves from her clothes.

"No one any of us knows," Carrick told them. "We'll send for the constable. Perhaps it's someone he's had a run in with."

She nodded.

"Smith and Willis will take care of the man. We'll go on to the manor so we can get the two of you under shelter."

"Thank you," Trixie gave him a weak smile.

"Are you all right?" Nathaniel asked. "I hope I didn't bruise you when I pushed you to the ground."

"I'm fine. Any cuts or bruises I might have received are far better than the alternative," she reminded him.

The muscle in his cheek jumped. "Indeed." He offered her his arm. "Still, I feel bad for the rough handling."

"No need." She gratefully took his arm for support. Her knees were more wobbly than she cared to admit. "A little soap and water for my hands and hot tea for my nerves and I'll be right as rain."

"Tea?" Carrick scoffed. "Brandy is what you need to settle the nerves."

She crinkled her nose. "Never developed a taste for brandy so I'll just stick with tea."

Carrick chuckled. "Your loss, my dear."

14

"**HAVE** we been invaded, sir?" Carrick's butler, held open the door when they arrived.

"No, Edgar, I'm afraid not. Just the one bugger. Andrew managed to get him right off." He handed his rifle to the elderly man and shed his coat.

"How disappointing for you. Shall I tell the boys to stand down?"

"I suppose so." Carrick's tone held genuine disappointment. He handed Edgar his coat in exchange for his gun. "Then again..." Carrick paused. "It might not be a bad idea to keep a look out posted through the night. Tell the boys to arrange it."

"Very good sir." Edgar's gaze finally settled upon Nathaniel. "Master Dennison. It's good to see you again. I hope you have been well."

"I have, Edgar. Thank you. You're looking well."

"I am, sir."

"Edgar, this is Miss Wadeworth." Carrick made the introductions. "Would you have Mrs. Jones prepare one of the guest rooms for her? I'm sure Nathaniel will be happy with his usual room."

"Of course, sir. And how long will they be staying?"

Carrick looked to Nathaniel.

"Probably just a day or two."

"Very good, sir." Edgar tipped his head. "Miss Wadeworth, Master Dennison, would either of you like to freshen up after your journey?"

"That would be lovely, thank you." Trixie smiled gratefully.

"This way Miss. I'll ring for Mrs. Jones."

"We'll be in the library," Carrick told Edgar. "Oh, and would you send someone up for Gerard? I'm surprised he didn't come down when the shots were fired."

"Yes, sir," Edgar told Carrick.

Carrick handed his gun to one of the men who had accompanied him. "Thank you, Samuel. Maybe next time we'll have better luck."

The men mumbled something and returned to their posts.

Nathaniel followed Carrick to the library.

"So what have you gotten yourself into this time?" Carrick asked as he poured them both a brandy.

"I'm not entirely certain." He recounted stumbling across Trixie in the London RIO, their flight to Edinburgh, as well as what little he recalled about Trixie's parent's disappearance. "And now her brother Peter has disappeared."

"Do you think someone wants Trixie as well?"

"It's possible. What I can't figure out is why."

"That's what I've been trying to work out as well," Trixie said when she joined them near the couch.

Both men sprang to their feet but she waved them back into their seats.

"If I may be so bold, Miss. Wadeworth, there are only three motivators behind any strategic maneuver. Power, money, and love."

She took a seat on the sofa near Nathaniel. "I don't know how my family could help anyone in any of those areas."

"You'd be surprised," Nathaniel said.

"Nathan said you were now running your father's business?"

"That's right," Trixie confirmed.

"If you don't mind me asking, how much is your company worth?" Carrick asked.

"To be honest, I couldn't name an exact figure of the company's worth from memory. We are largely debt free so it is a profitable business to be sure. But I can't see that anyone would want to kidnap or kill over it."

Nathaniel tipped his head. "Who would stand to inherit if something happened to both you and your brother?"

"Uncle George and then his eldest, Fitzgerald."

"Any animosity there?"

She shook her head. "None at all. Uncle George has done quite well with his textile mills. He supports many of the best dress makers in London and Edinburgh."

Both men made noises of slight interest then fell silent. Trixie poured herself a cup of tea from the tray that had been brought in while they had been chatting.

"Was your father working on any new projects or inventions at the time of his disappearance?" Nathaniel asked.

"Father was always working on something." Trixie smiled at the memory. She paused as she remembered a detail. "Now that I'm thinking about it, I do recall overhearing him and mother talking not long before they left on their journey that he had been disappointed when Lord Gathidy didn't respond to him about something."

"Gathidy was a former the Minister of Science, wasn't he?" Carrick asked Nathaniel.

"I believe so," Nathaniel confirmed.

"Any idea why Gathidy would be contacting your father?" Carrick asked.

She shook her head. "I'm afraid not."

"Would your father have written about something like that in his journal?" Nathaniel asked.

"I suppose it is possible." She shrugged. "But I can't read it."

Nathaniel raised a brow. "Couldn't open the lock after all?"

"No, it opened once I repaired one of the cogs some fool had bent. Unfortunately he wrote everything using one of his codes. I have been unable to make any sense of it."

"Do you mind if I take a look?"

"Not at all." She pulled the book from the pocket of her skirts and handed it to him. "Father loved to experiment with coded languages. He used to send us secret messages just to see if we could figure out what it said."

Nathaniel flipped through the pages. His interest peaked immediately. "This is quite good."

"Good, as in difficult to crack?" Carrick asked.

He glanced up from the book for a moment. "Oh definitely."

"But isn't that bad for us?" Trixie asked.

"Perhaps." Nathaniel grinned. "It will certainly provide a challenge for me."

"Perhaps now would be a good time to show you about the house then?" Carrick got to his feet and offered Trixie his arm. She glanced at Nathaniel then stood and took Carrick's offering. "And perhaps you could tell me all about your airship."

Their voices faded as they exited the study.

Nathaniel frowned at the book in his hands. The thrill of solving a new and obviously challenging puzzle had dimmed. Normally he would have lost all sense of those around him as he began to pick apart the pieces. The thought that Trixie would be spending time with Carrick, alone, hovered on the edge of his consciousness and irritated him greatly.

Carrick was one of his oldest and dearest friends. He trusted him implicitly. But where Trixie was concerned, doubts bubbled to the surface. Some primitive part of him didn't want other men near her. Not that Carrick would be anything less than a gentleman with her. But he didn't want anyone else showing her the ins and outs of the castle and reciting its history to her. It might be Carrick's castle but Nathaniel wanted to have that one-on-one time with Trixie.

Yet here he sat. With a book instead of the woman.

He needed to be careful. She had left him behind once. Who was to say she wouldn't do it again? Her leaving had hurt but he had gotten over it. Perhaps the trick was in not caring whether she was in or out of his life.

He grunted. Not caring. Could he manage that where she was concerned?

He moved to the desk and blocked out those uncomfortable thoughts and focused on the text in front of him. Finally the room faded and the words and symbols popped off the page. In his mind's eye he moved letters and numbers around and matched them with new ones. Before long words began to form. Eventually, whole sentences.

When he broke free of the cloud of letters and symbols, he found he had scribbled over multiple sheets of paper he had somehow taken from the drawer. Carrick and Trixie had returned from their walk and were watching him with interest.

"Did you enjoy your tour about the castle?" Nathaniel asked.

"And just like that he's back with us," Carrick murmured.

Trixie smiled. "I did."

"Dinner is about ready. Will you be joining us or disappearing into that book again?" Carrick asked.

Nathaniel reached for his pocket watch. "Is it time for supper already?" The rumble in his stomach confirmed it was.

"It is."

"Excellent." Nathaniel snapped the lid of his watch closed and sprang to his feet. He pocketed the journal then offered Trixie his arm. She took it and the three of them headed toward the dining room.

"Did you make any progress on Father's journal?" she asked.

"I did. Unless he switches methodology, I feel confident I can translate all of your father's notes."

"That's wonderful." She squeezed his arm. "I can't wait to read Father's words again."

The smile she gave him lit up her face and made him feel like a giant amongst men.

15

WHEN they arrived at the dining room they found a young man seated at the table with a glass of wine in one hand and a book in the other.

"Gerard. It's about time you left that dungeon you call a bedroom," Carrick said.

The young man looked their way. If he was surprised to see guests, he didn't act like it. "Mrs. Jones refused to send a tray up while there were guests in the house."

Nathaniel chuckled. "Terribly sorry to inconvenience you, old boy."

"A dammed nuisance is what it is," Gerard grumbled. "Had to put on clean trousers and everything."

"Master Jamison!" Mrs. Jones exclaimed as she entered the dining room. She set the tray she had been carrying on the sideboard and put her fists on her hips. "That kind of talk might be acceptable at your club or in the stable but not here. Especially not with a lady present. Your mother, God rest her soul, would be mortified to hear it."

Gerard sighed and got to his feet. He came around to their side of the table and took Trixie's free hand. "My apologies. I'm afraid I am so out of touch with polite society that my manners often slip." He bowed his head. "Do forgive me."

Trixie's lips twitched with amusement. "It's quite all right. My brother is much the same way after he has been locked away in his laboratory for too long. I am afraid he very nearly forgets how to properly use a spoon."

Mrs. Jones harrumphed and returned to the kitchens.

Gerard's eyes twinkled. "As you have already heard, dear lady, my name is Gerard Jamison."

Nathaniel quickly stepped in. "Gerard this is Miss Beatrix Wadeworth."

"A pleasure." Gerard squeezed her fingers then returned to his place at the table.

Trixie and Nathaniel exchanged amused glances when Gerard had to quickly correct himself and wait until Nathaniel had seated her before taking his own.

"So Gerard, may I inquire as to what you have been doing these past few days. I swear I don't think we've seen you in a week," Carrick asked while one of the serving ladies brought out the first course.

"Mostly research." Gerard fingered the edges of his book as if he couldn't wait to crack it open again.

"I assumed that much. But what about this time," Carrick pressed.

"I've been studying wings," Gerard admitted.

"Wings?" Nathaniel asked.

"Wings," Gerard confirmed.

Nathaniel glanced her way. She hid her grin behind her spoon.

"What kind of wings?" Carrick asked.

Gerard sniffed his soup. "Bird wings. Insect wings. I even managed to find a bat up in one of the attics."

"Mrs. Jones will throw a fit if there are a bunch of animals and bugs running around your room."

Gerard finished off his soup before everyone else. "No worries there. Everything I've brought in is dead."

The room went silent. The serving girl dropped the ladle into the tureen with a clang then with a gasp she hurried out of the room.

Trixie held her napkin to her lips to smother her laughter. Nathaniel shook his head and finished the last of his soup. Carrick muttered something under his breath and Gerard finally gave in to the temptation and flipped opened his book.

Despite Carrick's elevated status, the rest of their dinner was enjoyed with a complete lack of fanfare or ceremony. Carrick and Nathaniel took turns sharing stories of all the trouble they had gotten together either as children or at University. She could see how the two of them had grown so close.

Gerard contributed to the conversation when Carrick or Nathaniel pulled him in, but otherwise he simply listened and observed. His gaze frequently drifted her way.

She finally realized Gerard's attention wasn't on her but rather one of her mechanical friends. "Gerard, you are welcome to take a closer look at Nid." She encouraged the brass and silver spider upon her hand. "She's probably the calmest of my pets."

Gerard's face brightened. "They're... fascinating."

"You said your father created them?" Carrick asked.

"Yes. He worked on the idea for years, but didn't perfect the power source until just before he disappeared."

"The timing certainly raises a few questions with respect to your father's crashed airship," Carrick said.

"How did your father power these?" Gerard asked as he studied Nid.

"I... I don't really know. I've never questioned it." Trixie absently petted Squeaks who had come out of her hiding place. "Father only told me that as long as I kept their gears well maintained and wound them up at least weekly, they would be with me my entire life."

Carrick let out a low whistle.

"That's remarkable," Gerard mumbled as he examined the spider he had coaxed onto his hand.

"Have any of your pets gone missing?" Nathaniel asked.

"No. A couple have, well... died, for a lack of a better word."

Carrick's brows rose. "Died how?"

She shrugged. "One fell off the roof. He was so damaged that even Peter couldn't repair him."

"And the others?" Nathaniel prompted.

"Two of them we don't know what happened. They just stopped working. Peter tinkered with them and eventually dismantled them but he was never able to figure out what was wrong."

"What did you do with them?" Nathaniel asked.

"Like I said, Peter took them apart in an attempt to repair them. He's used many of the parts over the years to repair the others."

"So the parts have never gone missing," Carrick clarified.

She glanced from one man to the other. "Not that I know of. But in truth, I wouldn't know with any certainty. Given the condition of his workshop, I doubt even Peter would know."

The men exchanged meaningful looks.

"Would you mind if I took one of them apart?" Gerard asked.

Trixie gasped in alarm.

"No." Nathaniel's tone brooked no argument.

"Gerard, I don't think Trixie sees these as trinkets." Carrick said. "I suspect they are more valuable to her than a cherished pet."

"You would be correct," she told them.

"My apologies." Gerard gave her an awkward grin as he let Nid crawl back onto the table. "My curiosity got the better of me. I didn't stop to think that your father's creations might mean something more to you than the scientific genius that they are."

She tipped her head in acknowledgement even as she reached for Nid.

"We really need to get you out in society more often, brother," Carrick chuckled.

"Why would I ever want to do that?" Gerard said with mock horror.

Nathaniel shook his head.

"So that you can talk with women without upsetting them," Carrick said.

Gerard harrumphed.

"Perhaps we can find something in your father's journal

about them," Nathaniel said.

"Oh, yes." She scooted her chair closer when he pulled out the book so they could read at the same time.

Nathaniel gestured to the book. "You'll have to unlock it again. It appears to lock each time you close the cover."

"I'm surprised it didn't lock on you while you were working on it earlier," she said as she pulled her necklace out from underneath her blouse.

"I never closed it."

She placed the key on the lock mechanism. She twisted the key back and forth until the gears turned and unlatched the closure.

"Do you remember the date of when you father finished working on them?"

"He gave me the first one on my eighteenth birthday," she told him.

He thumbed through the pages until he landed on an entry dated around that time. Using a scrap piece of paper he pulled from the back of the book, he translated a few paragraphs while the rest of the group enjoyed dessert.

"I'm not sure this means anything." He pushed the paper to Trixie.

She scanned the hastily scribbled words. The entry referenced a luncheon he attended. She reread it to be certain of what it said. Her father would have never written about something so trivial. Especially not in this journal.

"What else does it say?" she asked.

"On the same entry or one of the days next to it?"

"Would it take long to do all three?"

Nathaniel scanned the pages. "Not long."

"Perhaps we should retire to the library?" Carrick suggested.

"A wonderful idea." Gerard pushed his chair back and got to his feet.

Trixie nodded her agreement.

In the library, Carrick and Gerard poured themselves a brandy. Nathaniel settled behind the desk while Trixie sampled the chocolates Carrick offered.

The boys were just helping themselves to another glass when Nathaniel held up a new piece of paper to her. She tugged the paper from his fingers. When she finished reading she looked up at him. Nathaniel had blanked his expression.

"What does it mean?" she asked for clarity.

"One of three things." Nathaniel lay the pen on the desk next to the papers he had been using. "Either it means exactly what it says, or your father changed just enough of the story to confuse anyone reading who wasn't present that day, or I made a mistake decoding your father's formula."

She reread the pages.

Carrick set a glass of brandy down in front of Nathaniel. "You never make mistakes when it comes to codes."

"So that only leaves two choices," Trixie murmured.

Carrick held his hand out to Trixie. "May I?"

She shrugged and handed him the papers.

Carrick's eyes skimmed downward and he flipped to the next page. "Do you really think your father felt that having tea with someone named…" He squinted at the paper. "Named R. Layot was so memorable that he needed to write it down?"

She grimaced. "No."

Carrick tossed the papers onto the desk. "That eliminated the first."

"Which leaves us with the second theory," Nathaniel said.

"So who is R. Layot and why was their meeting important?" She waited for Nathaniel or Carrick to offer answers, but both responded with blank looks.

16

"**EARLIER** this month I was asked to investigate a string of disappearances," Nathaniel confessed to their group. "Each one has occurred in the last six months. And it seems that all of the missing persons are connected in some way to a recent invention or scientific discovery." He pulled his notebook from his jacket pocket and thumbed to the page he wanted. "However, after reviewing Investigator Morris' notes in the Edinburgh office, I think the disappearances have been going on a lot longer than the RIO realized."

Trixie frowned. "There is a whole list of people who went missing with no witnesses to their disappearance or clues to why they left?"

"Basically," Nathaniel said.

"So, just like Peter," she pointed out.

"Yes."

She flinched.

"Who's Peter?" Gerard asked.

"My brother." Trixie got up and went to the window.

"I'm sorry. To clarify, is her brother one of the men on this list?" Gerard asked Nathaniel softly.

"No." Nathaniel told him. "Neither is her father." He kept one eye on Trixie as he continued. Her back was ramrod straight as she stared out into the night. "There have been no ransom notes delivered, no evidence of suicide or illicit affairs. All of these people have just vanished. Almost overnight." Nathaniel told the men.

"And you said they were all scientists?" Gerard asked.

"That's how it appears. I don't know most of the names on the list so I plan to reach out to a friend of my sister's when I returned to London. I think I need an expert in the scientific community."

"Or someone who follows all the journals and occasionally attends the lectures?" Gerard asked.

Nathaniel raised a brow. "That might do." He handed Gerard the list of names he'd collected from Mr. Morris' files.

Without a word, Trixie rejoined their group. Nathaniel leaned across the desk and squeezed her hand to offer a small measure of support.

"These I know." Gerard pointed to four of the names on the list. "Let me check something." He went to one of the bookcases and removed three books. He dropped them onto the desk. The books were different volumes of the same scientific journal.

Gerard flipped open the cover and skimmed the table of contents. "I thought that name was familiar." He set the book down on the table where the rest of their group could see. His finger lay next to a name that matched one on the list. "I haven't read a lot about him, because I don't care much about his field of study, but I knew I had read something about him."

"What about the others?" Nathaniel asked.

Gerard shrugged. "Can't hurt to look."

Nathaniel and Trixie flipped open the covers of the other books.

"I don't see any of the names in this one," Nathaniel said.

"I believe this one has two of the names." Trixie pointed out two names in the list against the contents of the journal she had.

"Do you have any other books?" Nathaniel asked.

"Of course. Same shelf." He pointed to one of the bookcases. "And I have a few more in my room."

Within the other books they found all but one of the names on the list.

"Other than publishing a paper in the same journal do these

people have anything in common?" Trixie asked.

Gerard mumbled, "Varying backgrounds, education." He continued reading. "Although, if I remember correctly these three worked together on last year's Ministry Challenge to create a replacement for a butler." He circled the names with his finger.

"What is the Ministry Challenge?" Carrick asked.

"The Ministry of Science poses a challenge each year for anyone in the community to compete in. It's a different task each time and participants have six months to submit their solution. Participants may submit a written solution or a working prototype. The entries are evaluated and judged by a panel and the winner has their results published in the Journal of Science."

Trixie frowned. "That is a lot of work for a mention in a journal."

"There is a monetary award attached to it as well. To fund future research, of course."

Trixie nodded. "Ah. That makes more sense."

"So at least a few of these men knew each other," Nathaniel redirected them back to the original topic.

"Yes," Gerard confirmed. "And this group won the challenge that year." He circled the names on the list with his finger.

"They actually made a replacement butler?" Trixie asked.

"Not entirely. Their prototype couldn't do everything a butler did, but it was able to open doors, take your coat, and deliver drinks."

"Did you go to the presentations?" Carrick asked.

"I did."

"Do you know the men?" Nathaniel asked.

"I met them at the presentation but no, we're not on familiar terms."

"Do you know what the others were working on?" Nathaniel asked.

"Not off hand. But I'm sure their journal submissions will give us at least a hint."

After skimming each of the papers in Gerard's journals Nathaniel said, "So these men worked on either propulsion, alternate power sources, machines, or a combination of those."

"What are you thinking?" Trixie asked Nathaniel.

"I'm not sure."

"Perhaps you should sleep on it," Carrick gestured to the clock standing in the corner.

"Oh. I didn't realize it had gotten so late," Trixie said.

"Me either," Nathaniel agreed.

Carrick got to his feet. "I need to check in with James. Perhaps we can resume this discussion tomorrow after breakfast?"

"Agreed." Nathaniel gathered the papers they had been writing on and returned his notebook to his pocket.

"Oh, Carrick? Would it be possible to have a note sent to my housekeeper in London to let her know that I'm safe?"

"Certainly. Just leave whatever letter you want sent on the tray in the entryway. Edward will take care of it."

"Thank you so much," she said graciously.

Nathaniel offered Trixie his arm. "I'll walk you to your room."

She put her hand on his arm. "Good night, Carrick. Good night, Gerard."

The men bid her goodnight.

Nathaniel escorted her to the room she had been given. It was nice to not feel obligated to say anything as they strolled. At her door he hesitated. His room was in the hallway adjacent to hers, but once the house went cold and dark, it may as well be in the next county. "Will you be all right tonight?"

She took a deep breath. "Yes. Of course." She glanced into the room. "I assume Carrick has some measure of protection for the house."

"Naturally."

"Then we should be safe for the night."

"Yes, we should." He kissed the back of her hand. "I just want to make sure you're comfortable."

She lifted on her toes and pressed a kiss to his cheek. "I will be fine. Thank you for caring."

Her lips had been a distraction all day. The temptation to taste them once again was too much.

He lowered his head and kissed her softly, yet firmly. The feel of her soft curves when she sagged against him fueled his need for her. He slipped one hand around her waist and pulled her closer.

The way she grasped the front of his shirt spurred him on. He deepened their kiss by tracing the edges of her lips with his tongue until she opened up for him. She gasped when he touched his tongue to hers but quickly overcame her shock and began her own innocent exploration. His control slowly trickled away. He wanted nothing more than to push her up against the wall and ravage her mouth as well as her body.

He forced himself to end the kiss but her dazed expression fueled the fire burning within. He rested his forehead against hers and whispered, "I need to go."

"Why?" she whispered.

Every muscle in his body went rigid and he lifted his head. "Because if I don't I won't be content with just kissing you."

She bit her lip. "What if I am not content with just kissing either?"

He groaned. "You don't know what you're asking."

"Actually I do."

He frowned.

"Not in practice. But I know what happens between a man and woman. I've read plenty of books on the subject."

"Then you know the risks involved."

"Yes."

His mind went blank at the possibility of what she was offering. He glanced up and down the hallway and grimaced. "We cannot have this discussion here."

She pushed the door to her room open further. "Then come inside."

He ground his teeth. His body clamored for her but his mind insisted he shouldn't. Not without some understanding between them. After all, wasn't that how a gentleman behaved?

"No."

"Nathaniel, I'm not some indecisive miss hoping to land a titled husband." She pulled him inside her room and shut the door behind him. "You and I have known each other for years. We have danced around our feelings for each other more than once."

She emptied her pockets onto the desk - Nid, her father's journal, as well as a few scraps of paper - then faced him. "I understand you have hesitations. You may even feel that you are taking advantage of me and this situation." She loosened the buttons on her blouse as she spoke. "But I want you to know that I am not doing this on a whim. Nor am I attempting to trap you into marriage." She spread her hands out to the side. "You're the only man I have ever wanted. If I only have one chance to experience something this special, then I want it to be with you." She met his gaze. "Does that make sense?"

"Yes." He crossed the room and stood before her. "But I need you to understand something." He held her gaze. "If we do this thing, our relationship will forever be changed."

"Change for the better or the worse?"

He smirked. "Perhaps a little of both."

Her brow furrowed in question.

He slipped his arm around her waist and pulled her closer. "I never stopped caring about you, Trixie. Even when I didn't know where you were or why you'd left, I didn't stop."

Her lips parted with her swiftly indrawn breath.

"I strongly suspect that doing this will only make me want you more."

"Truly?" she whispered.

"Have I ever lied to you?"

She shook her head.

"I don't plan to start now."

He lowered his head and pressed his lips to hers. She sighed and slid her hands across his chest and up to his shoulders. Her body softened as she clung to him. Her delicate curves fit his hard lines in all the right places and heightened his need for her.

After loosening the last few buttons on her blouse, he pushed it off her shoulders. The garment fell to the ground behind her, forgotten. With anything except maidenly shyness, she tugged his shirt loose from his breeches and began her own exploration. Her tiny hands distracted him as much as they inflamed him.

He backed her up until her legs hit the edge of the bed then he toppled her backwards onto the mattress. Her eyes widened and her breath caught when he came to rest between her legs. His erection pressed against her, making it abundantly clear just how much he desired her.

She reached for his belt but he grabbed her hands and pinned them above her head.

"What—" she wiggled and tried to pull her hands free.

"I'm not finished with you yet," he explained.

"But I want to touch you."

"There will be time."

He skimmed the tips of his fingers down the side of her face, her neck, then onto her chest. With deliberate slowness, he pulled on the ribbon that held her chemise together. The thin fabric fell open but not enough to satisfy him. He tugged the opening aside until he revealed her breast.

With all the reverence due a queen, he lowered his head and sampled the pink bud. She gasped as soon as his lips made contact. He drew circles around the pebbled nub with his tongue. Her back arched as if pleading for more.

After fumbling with the buttons on her riding skirt he made the mistake of releasing her hands. As soon as she realized she was free she lunged for him. She pulled and tugged at his jacket trying to free him, even as she greedily devoured his lips. Her urgent demands heightened his need.

With a muttered curse, he sat up, shrugged out of his jacket, and flung it aside. Then he worked enough of the buttons on his shirt free so he could pull it over his head. It soon followed his jacket. Her hands were on him before he could even draw breath. He resisted her tugs and pulls and finished loosening her skirt so he could slide it and her pantaloons down her legs, out of the way.

"Scoot up and lay your head on the pillows," he instructed. Once she complied he touched each of her ankles and slowly worked his way upward. When he reached her knees, he applied gentle pressure to urge her to open for him. Using only one finger, he touched her core. She was warm and wet for him. His cock throbbed with anticipation.

Unable to resist the temptation lying before him, he leaned forward and pressed his lips to her opening. She shrieked in surprise and tried to scoot away but he held her firmly by the hips. Soon enough she gave herself over into his attentions. He alternated between licking and suckling at the tiny nub that drove her pleasure. She whimpered and squirmed yet he didn't relent. When he pressed one finger into her opening she stiffened and her breathing paused. With one more flick on that sensitive bud, she cried out her release.

Her body shook as he lapped at her center. When she finally relaxed from the rush he leaned back gazed at her. She was exquisite. Her eyes were closed and her breaths came in short gasps for air. Tiny drops of moisture dotted the middle of her chest.

"Trixie look at me," he told her softly.

Her eyes fluttered open. The tenderness and awe he found there made his heart swell. "I want you here with me, aware of what is happening, when I join with you."

She nodded.

He guided his cock to her entrance then fraction by fraction, sank deeper inside of her. Her tight sheath was heaven. The urge to ride her hard and fast strained his control but he was determined to make it as painless for her as he could. When he reached her maidenhead he stopped.

"This may hurt a little. I promise to make it quick then do everything I can to make it feel wonderful again."

She nodded again. "I trust you."

He captured her lips then with one quick thrust pushed through the barrier. She flinched and all of her muscles stiffened. He rained kisses across her face and down her neck as he palmed her breast.

"Are you okay?"

"Yes. It only hurt a little."

"I'm sorry. It will be better again."

She nodded. "It's an odd feeling having part of you inside of me."

"Odd in a good or bad way?"

"Other than that one part, good. I like being this close to you."

Pride swelled within him even as he struggled to ignore the throbbing in his groin. "Good because I really like being this close to you too."

He kissed her again to show her just how much. Then he licked his way down to her breast. When he drew the tip into his mouth she grasped his head and pulled him closer. Taking it as a sign that her discomfort had faded, he began to move inside of her. Ever so slowly he rocked back and forth. Her hands slid across his back and she moaned.

He pulled her leg up and encouraged her to wrap it around his hips. Then he picked up their tempo. With the new angle, the walls of her channel gripped him even tighter. The need to come became insistent. He adjusted his position so he could reach between their bodies and touch her sensitive bud.

It only took a few strokes of his finger to send her over the edge. Her legs began to shake then she stiffened beneath him. Her pleasure spilled over, urging him to let go. With a hoarse cry into her neck he also found his release.

For a moment he could see nothing but stars behind his eyes. When he was finally able to put two thoughts together he rolled to the side to avoid crushing her but kept her within the circle of his arms.

As they both struggle to catch their breath she murmured, "I believe that is even better than flying in my airship."

He chuckled and pulled her closer against him. "I do believe you are correct."

And for a moment all was right with the world.

17

AN explosion echoed in the night.

Trixie opened her eyes and forced the haze of sleep aside. Nathaniel sat on the edge of the bed, buttoning his shirt.

"What's going on?" she asked.

"I'm not sure but I'm going to find out."

"I'll come with you."

"No." He put his hand on her hip to still her movements. "Stay here. It's the middle of the night. The house will be cold and dark. Most likely the only ones who will be about will be Carrick and the guards." He retrieved her bag and pulled out her pistol as well as Wings. "You will be safe here but keep these with you just in case." He set them on the table next to the bed.

He buttoned his pants but didn't bother tucking his shirt. After pulling on his boots, he grabbed his jacket and kissed her quickly on the lips. "Lock the door after I leave and don't open it for anyone except for me or Carrick. Understood?"

She nodded. "Be careful."

He gave her a cheeky grin. "Always am."

After the door clicked shut, she scrambled out of the bed and secured the lock. A chair butted up against the door would make it more secure but it also made her feel foolishly alarmed.

She donned the robe she found lying across the back of a chair. It was several sizes too big, but better than nothing. Whatever had woken them was likely nothing. They would be able to go back to sleep as soon as Nathaniel returned so it seemed pointless to dress.

She curled up on the bed and pulled the blanket over her. Would he stay with her through the rest of the night?

Her body grew warm. Her introduction to the pleasures of the flesh had been... most enjoyable. Nathaniel made it everything she had hoped for. He had been gentle and saw to her fulfillment. Everything she had read on the subject warned that the first time would be painful but he had taken care to minimize her discomfort.

Perhaps she would have a chance to explore the things that would give him pleasure when he returned. She tried to recall the things she had read about what men liked. Before long her eyes began to droop. Someone knocking on her door woke her.

"Trixie, it's me."

"Nathaniel?" Trixie asked as she fumbled with the key in the lock.

"Yes." The weariness in his voice came through in the one syllable.

She pulled the door open and stepped back so he could enter. "What happened?"

His eyes drifted down the front of the robe as he passed. "You need to get dressed."

She closed the door and followed him further into the room. "Why?"

He wiped a hand over his face and faced her. "There's been another attack."

She moved closer. "Is anyone hurt?"

"One of the stable boys."

"Not badly, I hope."

He handed her blouse and skirt to her. "Some burns and likely a broken arm. The bump on the back of his head is what concerns them. He was out cold for a while."

She found her chemise and pantaloons. "Is there something you need me to do for him? I have some knowledge of injuries."

"No. Nothing like that." He waved for her to go ahead and

dress. "There's someone asking to speak with you."

She grasped the front of the robe and frowned at him. "Who would show up here, at this time of night, asking to speak to me?"

"That's just one of the many things we'd like to know," he groused. "Please hurry. I can only look at you in that robe for so long before I decide that this man's questions can wait until tomorrow."

She blinked uncomprehending at him.

"You're not wearing anything under that, are you?" he asked.

She bit her lip. "No."

"And that is a bed right behind you, correct?"

She glanced over her shoulder. "Yes."

"In my book, the two naturally go together."

A fission of heat rippled through her body. "Yes, well..." She cleared her throat.

"But Carrick and the others are expecting me to return with you in a reasonable timeframe so we had best be moving."

She tried to hurry and dress but having someone watching her made her fumble with the buttons.

Nathaniel came to her aid. A maid was one thing, but having a gentleman around took some getting used to.

To expedite things, she pulled her hair back into a neat braid and pined it out of the way. Then she slipped her boots on. "I'm ready," she told him.

"That was remarkably fast." He got up from where he had perched at the edge of the bed and joined her. "I don't think my mother or sister have ever dressed that quickly."

She shrugged. "It is the middle of the night. We're not going to be presented to the Queen, so I don't see much point in making a fuss over my appearance."

"There's no need." He kissed her lightly on the lips and lingered for just a moment. "You're beautiful either way."

She beamed at his praise. "Thank you."

Before leading her out he made sure the hallway was clear. As they hurried through the passageways she asked, "What was the loud noise that woke everyone earlier?"

He grimaced. "Nothing but bad news."

She frowned. "About what?"

He stopped walking and faced her. "The *Valkyrie*."

"My ship?" Her voice cracked.

"I'm afraid so. We think the men we found ignited something aboard the ship. I'm afraid very little of it will be salvageable."

The ship Peter had designed for her was gone. Her parents were gone. Peter was gone. If they didn't find him, she would be all alone. She wobbled on her feet. He took her by the arm and steadied her.

"But I don't—" Her eyes narrowed. "It's the same people who have been following us, isn't it?"

A muscle flexed in his jaw. "We think so. We captured one of them. Carrick is holding him below stairs."

"Is that who wants to speak to me?"

"Yes," Nathaniel growled.

"I see." She was tired of being a pawn in someone's little game. It was about time that she found out who the puppet master was. She lifted her chin. "Take me to him."

"You don't have to go down there."

"I do if I want to know who is behind these attacks. It's likely related to Peter's disappearance." She held his gaze. "You think so as well, don't you?"

His lips were pressed into a line but he gave her a quick nod.

"Then let's see what this man has to say." She gestured for Nathaniel to go ahead.

He took her hand and led her to a set of stairs just inside the kitchens. She followed him down to a storage area. There were shelves of food and canned goods as well as bags of flour. Further along the way they passed a wine cellar. In the dim lighting she lost count of the number of doorways they passed. Finally they came to one that had been brightly lit by lamps and candles. In the center of the room a man she had never seen before sat tied to a chair.

From the number of cuts on his face and the tattered

condition of his clothes, the man had been in a recent scuffle. Carrick, Gerard, and a handful of Carrick's men stood nearby glaring at the man.

As soon as he spotted them in the doorway, Carrick stood and met them partway. "Do you know this man?" he asked, gesturing over his shoulder.

"No." She shook her head. "He doesn't look familiar at all."

"You're certain?" Carrick pressed.

She took a few steps closer. "Quite certain."

"He has been rather insistent upon seeing you," Carrick told her.

The man lifted his head. "You're Beatrix Wadeworth?"

"Maybe she is and maybe she isn't." One of Carrick's men leveled a pistol on the man. "Perhaps you'd like to tell us why you want to know."

The man squinted up at her through his swollen eye. "Yeah, you're Wadeworth's daughter. You favor him just a bit."

Trixie inched closer. "What difference would it make if I was?"

"We know you have the book," the man told her.

"What book?" she asked.

He looked at her as if she were daft. "Your father's journal, of course. If you want to see your brother alive, you will return to London and await further instructions. You have two days to comply."

"Why should I believe you?"

"My employer is not a man to be trifled with. If you are difficult he will send evidence of your brother's stay with him. Trust me when I say you won't like the evidence and yet you won't be able to refute it."

She marched forward before anyone could stop her and slapped the man across the face. "Where is Peter and what do you want with him?"

The man simply grinned. "I want nothing to do with him but my employer is an entirely different matter. You have two days."

The man's mouth twitched then he tossed his head back.

Carrick brushed past her. He grabbed the man's head and fought to pry his mouth open. Within seconds the man's mouth filled with foam and his body jerked with spasms.

"Dammit," Carrick swore.

Trixie stumbled backward. "What's wrong with him?"

"Poison," Nathaniel answered.

Carrick's lip curled in disgust as he wiped his hands on his trousers.

The man slumped to one side.

"What…?" Trixie's eyes widened in horror. "Is he dead?"

Nathaniel pressed two of his fingers against the man's neck then nodded.

She swallowed the bile that had risen in her throat.

"Well, at least we know that Peter is still alive," Nathaniel said.

"For now," Gerard added.

Nathaniel and Carrick scowled at Gerard.

Trixie took a deep breath and stiffened her spine. "Now what?"

"Now we make plans to return to London," Nathaniel told her.

Her voice fell flat. "So you think I should just turn over father's journal to them."

"No. Unless that is the only way to save Peter."

"Then I suggest you get busy extracting everything you can from that book while you can," Carrick suggested.

"Agreed." Nathaniel reached for Trixie's hand.

She resisted his tug. "Don't we need to set out for London?"

"Yes, but leaving in the middle of the night is beyond foolish. For all we know his friends are waiting for us on the road outside the estate. We will be better off resting tonight, making a plan for travel tomorrow, and finding out what is in your father's journal in between. After all someone is willing to kidnap and die for this book." He cast a meaningful glance at the man still tied to the chair.

"I'll make arrangements to get us to London," Carrick said.

Nathaniel raised a brow. "Us?"

"You don't think I'm about to miss out on all the excitement, do you?" Carrick said.

Nathaniel chuckled.

"I suppose you're going to make me stay here and hold down the fort?" Gerard grumbled.

"Not at all." Carrick slapped Gerard on the shoulder. "I say we make it a family outing."

Gerard's grin widened. "Excellent. I'll notify Mrs. Jones we'll be leaving for London as soon as possible."

"Very good." Carrick faced Nathaniel and Trixie. "I assume Nathaniel told you about your airship?"

She cringed. "He did."

"I'm sorry. But since it is now out of the equation do you have any preferences for transportation?"

Trixie looked to Nathaniel.

"Train would be faster than carriage. And with the four of us traveling together, perhaps safest too." Nathaniel suggested.

Trixie nodded her agreement.

"I'll see to it," Carrick told them. "I have a bit of estate business to settle in the morning. But if we're able to make the proper arrangements, we may be able to leave late in the afternoon. I believe there is a late train we could catch that runs into London."

Nathaniel tipped his head toward the dead man. "What about him?"

"The Constable is expected in the morning for the other man. We'll just add this one to his inquiry."

Trixie crinkled her nose. "Does that mean we'll have to answer questions?"

"Probably not. I know the constable well. Once he sees the evidence and talks with my men, he'll be able to put together the pieces. I'll let him know you're a RIO Investigator and that a complete report will be filed when you return to London. That should satisfy him."

"Good." Nathaniel reached for Trixie's arm. "I'm going to escort her back upstairs. Do you need me for anything else this evening?"

"No," Carrick waved them on. "I'll have the men double the watch until dawn. You should get what sleep you can. It's likely to be a long trip tomorrow."

"You need to rest, too," Trixie reminded him.

"I'll sleep when I'm dead." Carrick gave her a wink then rejoined his men.

18

THE next morning Trixie woke to an empty bed. Nathaniel had indeed returned to her room with her but didn't make love to her again. She'd been disappointed but heeded his warning that she would be tender since it had been her first time. He had made up for it by holding her all through the night.

Being cocooned in his arms had been the only reason she had fallen asleep. Worry for Peter had plagued her ever since they left the storeroom. Nathaniel probably sensed it and somehow he'd managed to make her feel protected. Even cherished.

Her emotions fluttered like kite in a storm. Her night with Nathaniel bordered on magical. If not for all of the danger and intrigue, it would have been. However her fears for everyone's safety continued to plague her – most especially for Peter. Then right on the heels of her fear came her anger at whoever wanted to harm them. In direct conflict to all of that, she was oddly excited by the adventure their trip had turned into. The mystery behind the danger intrigued her and she was determined to solve it.

By the time she finished washing and dressing she had pushed those feelings aside so she could focus on the things she could do something about. Then she headed downstairs to the library to learn what the men had planned for the day.

She found Nathaniel at the desk decoding her father's journal. He was so wrapped up in his work that he didn't even notice her approach the desk. "Good morning."

He looked up from his notes. At first his eyes were distant but as soon as they focused on her he smiled. "Good morning." He reached for her hand then pulled her to him for a tender kiss.

She blushed. "I see you're hard at work already."

"Yes. I hope you don't mind that I borrowed your key to unlock the journal." He set the pen aside and pulled her onto his lap. "I agreed with Carrick's suggestion about decoding what we could before we reach London, but I didn't want to wake you."

"No, I don't mind. I trust you."

He kissed her again and set her pulse to racing.

"Are you ready to go home?"

"Yes and no. Other than the attacks on our lives, I've enjoyed being with you. I worry it won't be the same when we return to London."

"It won't but—

A commotion in the hall had Trixie leaping off Nathaniel's lap. She prayed her pinkened cheeks didn't incriminate her. They turned toward the door in time for Carrick to breeze into the room.

"Ah, good. You're awake."

"Good morning, to you too, Carrick," Trixie said.

"Yes, yes. Good morning." Carrick waved the formalities away. "I was coming to ask Nathaniel a question about you."

"Oh?" She raised one brow.

"Do you ride?"

"Yes, but if you're asking in preparation for our journey, I feel I must warn you that I haven't much experience riding long distances." She grimaced. "We've always lived in London so I usually walk or take a coach. I am far more comfortable aboard an airship than horseback."

Nathaniel asked Carrick, "I don't suppose you gave in and had your coach repaired, did you?"

Gerard snickered as he strode into the room. "Finally."

"Aunt Patricia came for an extended visit a few months ago so I was forced to for her sake," Carrick grumbled.

Nathaniel chuckled. To Trixie he added, "It has been a long-standing joke that the day he began using his coach would be the day he picked out his burial spot."

She quickly reassured Carrick. "I can ride."

"You can use the carriage," he assured her. "Nathaniel can ride with you. Gerard too, if he prefers. But I'll ride with my men." He shrugged. "It might make the trip safer for you anyway."

"I suppose it makes sense to assume the attacks have been about me," she said.

The men exchanged glances.

"That is the most logical conclusion," Nathaniel said slowly. He reached for her hand. "But now that their message has been delivered they may back off."

"Not an assumption I will be making," Carrick said. "Now, if you'll excuse me, I'll see to the rest of the preparations." He paused. "Oh, Gerard, Warrick will be here at noon."

"I take it that you wish for me to attend?" Gerard asked.

"Yes. But we won't be reviewing the accounts until after lunch." Carrick shook his head. "That old codger knows just when to show up to finagle a meal."

"Perhaps that's why we thought he was a distant relative for so many years."

Carrick chuckled. "Maybe so." He sailed out of the library.

"Gerard, I was about to seek out Mrs. Jones for a tea tray for Trixie. Would you like anything?"

"Please. I missed breakfast so anything to tide me over to luncheon."

Nathaniel squeezed Trixie's hand. "I'll be right back."

She gestured to the desk. "May I review what you've already translated?"

"It's your book so I don't see why not."

She nodded then went to the desk to see what Nathaniel had done. There were several pages already transcribed. From the corner of her eye, she watched Gerard move from one bookshelf to another.

When he set a stack of six or seven books on the table she

asked, "Are you planning to take all of those to London?"

"I am." He sat on the couch and propped his feet up on the ottoman. "The library in the London place is nothing in comparison to this."

"I would think not. From what little I have seen in detail, this is a wonderful collection. I could happily spend years in here and not be able to read everything."

"That's probably true. I have certainly made an effort."

Nathaniel returned and joined her at the desk. "Anything of the notes stand out to you?"

She smiled up at him. "Not so far." Every time she looked at him she had flashes of moments from their lovemaking. Her cheeks grew warm along with other parts of her body.

His lips twitched as if he could read her mind. "Perhaps you could assist me with the decoding?"

"I'd love to. How can I help?"

"I can read the decoded words out loud if you'll write them down," he suggested.

"I can do that."

As they worked, Mrs. Jones arrived with the tea tray. Nathaniel took it from her and carried it to the desk. Trixie poured for herself and Nathaniel.

"Gerard, would you care for tea or biscuits? Mrs. Jones sent a few slices of ham and cheese as well."

"Excellent." He pulled a chair up to the desk.

They snacked and decoded pages for a couple of hours until Edward announced that Mr. Warrick had arrived. Gerard excused himself. Not long after Edward came to tell them that lunch would be served in the dining room shortly.

Lunch was a short informal affair due to the number of chores Carrick needed to handle before they could leave. As soon as they finished eating, Carrick, Gerard, and Mr. Warrick headed to the study while Nathaniel and Trixie returned to the library.

Once they were alone again he asked, "How are you feeling today?"

"Fine." Realization of what he was truly asking set in. She

blushed. "Oh. Yes, I am fine. I admit to being relieved to be able to ride in the carriage today though."

"I suspected that would be a better option for you." He kissed the back of her hand. "I wish I could tell you that you'll be perfectly safe during the trip but you are far too intelligent for that. I can assure you that Carrick will take every precaution at his disposal. His men are dedicated and well trained."

"Well trained in what?"

"Carrick took a different route in his service to the crown. Since he had two older brothers in line to assume the title he believed he was in a position to take more dangerous missions during the war. Many of the men you see here are old comrades who needed employment, and quite frankly, a place to recover."

"I see."

"They're all good men. And quite loyal to Carrick. I believe we will both be in good hands."

"That does ease my mind. Thank you."

They spent a delightful couple of hours working on the journal and made a surprising amount of progress despite the number of deliberate and not so deliberate touches and heated glances.

Finally Carrick came and announced their readiness. "Samuel is overseeing the preparation of the horses. We can leave within the hour if everyone is in agreement."

Trixie tipped her head. "My things are packed. I would just need a few moments to freshen up."

"Excellent. Nathaniel, I assume you can be ready in time?"

"Certainly. What can I do to help?" Nathaniel asked Carrick.

"Everything is well in hand. I assume you be joining Beatrix in the carriage?"

Nathaniel glanced her way. "Yes, if that's all right with you?"

"I would appreciate the company."

"Very good. I'll return when everything has been prepared," Carrick told them.

"I suppose we should go up and get our things," she suggested.

"Yes." He took her hand and helped her to her feet. "Carrick gets rather impatient. We wouldn't want to be the reason for a delay."

He escorted her up the stairs then paused as if he wanted to say something. The look in his eye sent shivers of delight through her. For a moment she thought he might follow her to her room but instead he told her, "I'll meet you in the library shortly."

She frowned. If he hadn't been so attentive to her in the library she might have thought he had been disappointed by their lovemaking. Perhaps he decided there wasn't enough time before they needed to leave for any kind of interlude. She was far too new at these things to know for certain but some of the more scandalous stories whispered about the ton made it sound as if couplings occurred rather quickly in some of the strangest locations.

If they ended up in the coach alone, she would ask him about it.

19

CARRICK joined Trixie, Nathaniel, and Gerard in the library. "Everything is ready. Your bags are already in the carriage." The four of them headed to the stable yard. Some of Carrick's men were already in the saddle. Others were checking the tack on their mounts.

Nathaniel handed Trixie up into the carriage then gestured for Gerard to proceed him.

He glanced back at the solid walls of Carrick's ancestral home. More than once he'd been tempted to lock Trixie inside while he looked for Peter. The only thing stopping him from doing so was the knowledge that she would never forgive him. Especially if anything did happen to Peter. So, for now, they would let the villain's game play out.

With one last salute to Carrick he climbed into the box. Gerard had claimed the corner opposite to Trixie so Nathaniel opted to sit beside her. He gave her a reassuring smile as they waited for the rest of the group to mount up.

Within minutes they were rolling away from the estate.

"Do you have the journal?" Nathaniel asked once he took his seat.

"Of course." She patted her skirt where the pocket lay.

"Once we exit the manor grounds I'd like to put that into the hidden compartment."

"Carrick has a hidden compartment in his carriage?"

"Of course."

"What ever for?"

"We don't ask a lot of questions in this family," Gerard said blandly.

Trixie looked to Nathaniel. "It is handy to have an out of sight place to store weapons or even a bottle of spirits." He added, "Just in case."

As soon as they crossed the estate boundary the landscape changed into large open fields. Nathaniel gestured to Trixie. "Let's put that journal away now."

She handed it over without question.

Gerard swiveled his feet up onto the bench. Nathaniel pressed a hidden latch in the wood paneling and popped open a small drawer. Inside the drawer lay a pistol wrapped in linen and a handful of banknotes. He dropped it in, closed the drawer, and then verified the latch held.

Gerard closed his eyes and presumably fell asleep once again.

Trixie whispered to Nathaniel, "Is he one of those people who prefers the night?"

Nathaniel chuckled. "Seems so."

"Peter goes through phases like that. When he's onto something with his research he often gets his days and nights mixed up. I can go days without seeing him upright."

He frowned. "Doesn't that get lonely?" He didn't like the idea that she spent more time alone than with what was left of her family.

"A bit at home. But I have a lot of interaction with people at the port so it's not as if I'm completely cut off."

"That's true."

He took her hand in his and stared out the window. Being here with her was right. Despite the hint of danger in the air, peace crept into his soul. What did it mean?

Perhaps after they found Peter and solved this puzzle he would explore it.

They rode in comfortable silence for some time. Trixie's head rested against his shoulder until a shout from one of the men outside of the carriage caught their attention.

"What's going on?" she asked.

"I'm not certain." Nathaniel scooted to the window but he couldn't see anything other than passing landscape. Trixie shifted closer to the other one.

There were more shouts outside.

"Gerard. Wake up." Nathaniel slapped Gerard on the knee.

"Hmmm? What?"

"Man that window."

Gerard didn't even question the command. He slid over, forcing Trixie to scoot to the interior so he could get close to the door.

"What's going on out there?" Trixie asked from right behind him.

"I'm not certain. The most logical estimation is that we're either being pursued or someone has attacked one of the men."

"Billie hasn't changed speed," Gerard pointed out.

"And we haven't altered course since the alarm was shouted," Nathaniel added.

"That's good, right?" Trixie asked.

The men exchanged glances.

"Probably," Nathaniel told her.

More shouts came from outside then a gun fired.

"Get down," Nathaniel ordered her.

She slouched in the seat. "Get down where?"

He pulled a pistol from beneath his jacket. "In the floor." His heart beat against his chest. Normally he relished the excitement of engaging the enemy. This time, fear licked at his consciousness. The fear wasn't for himself, but for Trixie. And it was dammed distracting.

Almost in sync the men lowered the glass windows in the doors. Gerard pulled his pistol from the holster. Both men readied their weapon near the windows.

"See anything?" Nathaniel shouted above the wind.

"Only Jacob and Isaiah. You?"

"No."

Trixie started to climb back up onto the seat but Nathaniel pushed her back down. "Stay down until we know what's going on," he growled.

"But I can't see anything."

"You don't need to," he said harsher than he'd intended.

"But—"

"No buts." The possibility of being shot never bothered him, but just thinking a stray bullet could hit her made his stomach clinch.

"Here comes Carrick," Nathaniel told Gerard.

Carrick maneuvered his horse next to the carriage. He shouted through the window, "Two riders. We took them out. We'll regroup just ahead."

"Anyone hurt?" Nathaniel asked.

"Jonathan."

Nathaniel gave him a brisk nod.

Both Nathaniel and Gerard kept their weapons in their hand. When the carriage finally came to a stop Nathaniel told Gerard, "Stay with her."

Before she could protest Nathaniel slipped out of the carriage and slammed the door behind him. He needed a moment to control his emotions so he strolled to where Carrick and the other men had gathered to check on Jonathan.

When he returned he knocked on the side of the carriage so as to not startle Gerard. Through the window he told them, "You can get out but we're only stopping for a few minutes."

"Where's Carrick?" Gerard asked.

Nathaniel jerked his head toward the rear. "He's seeing to Jonathan."

"How bad?"

"Not very. He might have some trouble riding but he'll definitely live."

"Good." Gerard jumped down from the carriage and headed in the direction Nathaniel had indicated.

"I'd like to stretch my legs for a moment," she told Nathaniel.

He nodded and held his hand out to help her down. "Probably would be a good idea. Just don't stray far from the carriage. It will give you some cover if anyone else comes."

"All right." She paused when she stepped onto solid

ground. With a groan she straightened her back then twisted in each direction.

Nathaniel kept his hold of her hand. Her discomfort worried him. "Are you all right?"

"Yes. It's just been a while since I rode any distance in a carriage."

"I suppose travel by airship isn't so confining, is it?"

She grinned. "No, it's not." She took a few steps. "If you need to check on the men, go ahead. I'll just walk a bit right here." She gestured to the flat area in front of her.

He released her hand but stayed close as she walked. Leaving her unprotected just wasn't in him. "My priority is you. Carrick is seeing to the men."

She had only made a couple of laps when Carrick approached.

"How's Jonathan?" Nathaniel asked.

"He's fine. Once he gets a bottle of whisky in him, he won't even know he was wounded."

"He's not drinking it now, is he?" she asked. "Didn't you say we had a bit further to ride?"

"No. Just a wee sip. We poured more on the wound than into him," Carrick reassured her.

Carrick gestured for Nathaniel to step aside with him. "As far as we could tell there were two attackers. One was shot point blank. The other just wounded. Isaiah chased the wounded man down. He's now tied up on the back of one of the horses."

"Is that wise?"

"I assume you don't want to put him in the carriage with Trixie."

Nathaniel glared at Carrick. If it were up to him, she wouldn't be in the same county as one of the attackers. "Of course not."

"When we reach Keswick, Jonathan will take the man we captured to the constable," Carrick told Nathaniel.

"Are you sure he can manage if he's wounded?"

"He says he can manage. If we make sure the man is

unconscious, it definitely won't be an issue. Especially not the way he's tied up."

"All right. At least he'll be able to get to a surgeon quickly. How far to Keswick?" Nathaniel asked.

"Not even an hour on horseback. Less if you take the path across the meadow. Unfortunately, the carriage won't make it on that path and I don't want to send Jonathan across a wide open space alone with one of their men."

"Me either."

When they rejoined Trixie near the carriage Carrick said, "I hope you were not unduly stressed by that incident."

"Not unreasonably so. I'm just thankful no one else was hurt."

"So we all are." Carrick tipped his head. "I'll rejoin the men. We should be off momentarily."

"We'll be ready," Nathaniel reassured him. After Carrick walked away he said, "How much of our conversation did you overhear?"

Without a hint of remorse, she said, "Most."

He shook his head. "What am I going to do with you?"

She batted her eyes at him. "Perhaps the same that I do with you?"

He stepped closer and told her in a lower tone, "You have no idea what I'd like to do with you."

Her eyes dilated and her cheeks turned pink. "Perhaps you could enlighten me?"

"Perhaps I will." He looked to where Gerard was marching in their direction. "But not right now." He took a step back. "Gerard. Are you ready to reclaim your seat?"

"No, I was just coming to say that I will not be joining you. Jonathan will be riding up top with Clark. I'm going to take his mount until we reach Keswick."

"That sounds reasonable," Nathaniel said.

Gerard reached into the carriage and tucked two of his books into a storage compartment. The third book he slid into his jacket pocket. "There. Now you'll have the carriage to yourselves." He tipped his hat at Trixie.

"Be careful back there," she told Gerard as he walked away.

"Always am."

20

THE carriage pulled away at Carrick's signal.

While Gerard didn't take up any more room than Nathaniel, it was nice to have the space to themselves. She scooted closer and rested her head upon his shoulder.

He shifted and wrapped his arm around her back and pulled her firmly against his side.

"Do you mind if I ask you a question?" she asked.

"No, go ahead."

"I was curious about a point of, well… intimacy." His entire form became still. "What about it?"

"Does it always take a while for men to…" She waved her hand in the air hoping he might suggest the right word.

"To?"

"To find their pleasure."

"Why do you ask?"

"Well I have heard stories of couplings in odd places such as a theater box or a dark corner of a garden. But I am having a lot of trouble reconciling what I now know of the act to those stories. It seems to me that based on the physical exertion involved, the amount of noise made, and the time spent, those couples would have most certainly been caught in the act. I don't understand why anyone would take those kinds of risks."

He made a choking noise. "First, I should clarify that no, it doesn't usually take men long to reach completion. Last night, I held out because I believed it was important for you find your pleasure."

A ripple of warmth rushed through her. "That's most considerate of you."

The quick kiss he dropped on her lips made her heart flutter.

"Secondly," he continued. "Sometimes the need to be with someone overrides a person's better judgement. And quite frankly the risk of being caught can lend to the excitement and amplify the pleasure."

"It can?" She frowned. "I should think the people involved would be so worried about being discovered that they wouldn't enjoy the moment."

"You would be amazed by what you can block out when you're lost in pleasurable sensations with the right partner." He nuzzled her cheek. "If I didn't need to remain alert to threats and we weren't being escorted by a half dozen men I would demonstrate."

Disappointment settled in as she blinked back the erotic images his words had conjured. "This is probably not a good time to be doing something like that."

He put one finger under her chin and urged her to look at him. "That doesn't mean that I don't want you. I do. So much that I ache. But your safety must come before everything else."

"Thank you."

"Perhaps we could work on the journal to pass the time?" he suggested.

She nodded. "Yes. That would be good."

He retrieved the journal from the hidden drawer while she took out a pencil and sheets of paper from her bag. For the reminder of the journey they worked on entries. There were a lot of equations and formulas. Most made no sense at all. But something in that book had value.

Even if they couldn't figure out what that something was, they would have a copy in case the original were lost.

Like in the office their work was frequently interrupted with touches or kisses. By the time they arrived in Penrith she was ready to pull the shades over the windows and demand that he ravish her.

"We're almost there. You should probably straighten your…" He gestured to his own hair.

"Ah, yes." She blushed. "I suspect I do look a little, um…"

"Lovely. You look lovely, even when a bit tousled."

Her cheeks heated further. "Thank you." She tucked her blouse into her skirt then ran her fingers through her hair and repined a few loose strands. "There. That will have to do."

"As I said, lovely." He took her hand and kissed the top of it.

When the carriage stopped near the train station, Nathaniel climbed down. "Wait here for a moment."

She slipped the journal into her pocket and returned the papers to her bag.

"Carrick has sent one of the men ahead to purchase seats for us. Should only be a moment," Nathaniel told her when he returned.

Once the bags were unloaded and Carrick had issued instructions for the other men's return home, Nathaniel helped her down from the carriage. They walked to the train as a group. Trixie on Nathaniel's arm, Carrick and one of the men ahead of them, Gerard and three of the men behind.

Did the Queen feel this stifled when she went out in public? Their precautions were for her own good but they were quickly becoming tiresome. When they were safely ensconced in one of the private cars she breathed a sigh of relief. She loved being near Nathaniel but the extra space in the car was a blessing.

"I have to admit, I've never had the opportunity to ride in a private car," Nathaniel told Carrick as he evaluated the space. "This is rather nice."

Carrick poured himself a drink from the bar situated in the corner. "I don't usually request one but it was the only way to guarantee we remained together. It also added an extra degree of security due to fewer people milling about."

"Whatever your reason, I appreciate it very much," Trixie told him. "I'm just sorry you have been so inconvenienced."

Gerard scoffed. "We should be thanking you. Carrick gets frightfully out of sorts without something to shoot."

The other men muttered their agreement.

Trixie pressed her lips together to stifle her grin as she glanced at Nathaniel. He didn't bother to hide his chuckle.

Surprisingly, their ride to London passed without incident. Along the way they made plans for the night and the next morning. Carrick's men, Fletcher and Jacob, would go with Trixie. Samuel and Willis would go with Carrick and Gerard to Jamison Place to rest for the evening then take over the watch in the morning. Nathaniel planned to go to his townhouse to clean up and pack a fresh bag. He would return to Trixie's during the night when he would be less likely to be seen. The threat to her family justified having two men in the house for security purposes but if he were seen coming and going, Nathaniel's stay would set the town gossips aflutter.

She might have moved beyond caring what the ton said or didn't say, but Nathaniel's mother and sister were another matter. There was no reason either he or his family should suffer undue scorn or whispers because of her. So she agreed to a discreet approach for his sake.

Carrick promised to send out inquires on the missing scientists first thing in the morning. He would drop by Trixie's after lunch. They said their farewells before disembarking the train with their belongings. Willis managed to arrange for two hackneys quickly. As soon as she took her seat inside their train car, she pulled the shade away from the window. The flickering gas lamps on the street corners cast odd shaped shadows on the pedestrians. But it wasn't the shadows that made the hair on the back of her neck stand on end.

Trixie reached for Nathaniel's arm. "Nathaniel, there's a man watching us across the street. Do you know him?"

He leaned closer to the window. "What man?"

When she turned to point the man out, he had vanished. "Oh. He's gone now."

"What did he look like?"

She described him, including the suit and hat he wore.

"Doesn't sound like anyone I know. You didn't recognize him?"

"No. Something about him stood out. Like he was out of place."

"Your gut is right more than you realize. Listen to it." He searched out the window again. "Let me know if you spot him again."

She nodded and watched the people they passed. When they reached her home the men got out and checked the area before letting her out. Nathaniel escorted her to the door while Fletcher and Jacob kept an eye on the street behind them.

Mr. Ellison answered the door. "Miss Beatrix. The missus has been worried sick about you." He eyed the men behind her warily as he opened the door wider to admit her.

"I'm so sorry to have caused either of you any worry. My trip to Edinburgh was supposed to be a fast turnaround. Unfortunately, things didn't go as planned." She gestured. "You may remember Mr. Dennison?"

"Yes, of course." He bobbed his head to Nathaniel.

"This is Fletcher and Jacob. They are associates of a friend of Mr. Dennison's. They will be staying to help keep an eye on things."

"What sorts of things need an eye kept on them?" Mrs. Ellison asked as she came to the foyer.

Trixie greeted Mrs. Ellison with a hug. "Me, I'm afraid."

"What has happened? Did you learn anything about Peter?" Mrs. Ellison asked.

"Let's get the men settled then I'll explain everything," Trixie suggested.

"Very well," Mrs. Ellison reluctantly agreed. "Where should we put them?"

"Peter's room is likely too messy to be managed on short notice. Go ahead and use the guest room as well as my parents' room."

Mrs. Ellison blinked in surprise. "Very well." She motioned to her husband. "Mr. Ellison can show you where you'll be staying. The guest room is already made up but I'll need to put fresh sheets in the other room. I haven't changed those in months."

"Don't trouble yourself. I'm sure they're fine as they are," Fletcher assured her as they followed Mr. Ellison up the stairs.

"Nonsense." She hurried to the kitchens.

Once they were alone, Nathaniel took her hand. "I'll be back. Tell Fletcher to look for me at about eleven. Which room is yours?"

"My window faces the east. At the top of the stairs turn left. It's the third door down the hall."

He kissed the back of her hand. "Don't lock your door," he whispered.

She shivered with anticipation. "Please be careful."

"I will."

He let himself out the main door leaving her alone in the foyer feeling somewhat discombobulated. She took a deep breath. The strain of the last couple of days wore heavily on her. Despite sitting all day, she wanted nothing more than a bath and to sleep in her own bed.

Since Mrs. Ellison was busy she put a pot of water on to warm in the kitchen then went to her father's office to lock the journal away. That task done, she gathered the things she'd need for a bath and carried them up to her room. When she went back downstairs for the heated water she found Mrs. Ellison waiting for her.

Over a cup of tea she told Mrs. Ellison everything that she had learned about Peter's disappearance, the attacks she and Nathaniel had endured, and how Carrick came to be involved.

While Mrs. Ellison flitted about the kitchen, Trixie's mind wandered. Had Nathaniel made it home safely?

"You poor dear," Mrs. Ellison shook her head. "You must be exhausted to be woolgathering like so." She wrapped the jug of hot water in a towel. "Take yourself upstairs. You look as if you need a good night's rest." She shooed Trixie toward the stairs. "I'll bring this up so you can wash up. Then off to bed with you."

When they reached her room, Mrs. Ellison poured some of the hot water into the basin then set the jug on the floor near the door. "I'll fetch your used water in a bit."

"Don't trouble yourself. I can bring it down in the morning after I wake."

Mrs. Ellison harrumphed. "Good night then." At the door Mrs. Ellison paused. "I'm glad you made it home safely. Please make an effort to take care of yourself."

"I will."

21

NATHANIEL waited in the shadows until he found Fletcher making a patrol outside of Trixie's home.

Fletcher showed Nathaniel where to enter at the back then moved along with his watch.

The house was dark but he knew enough of the layout to make his way upstairs. He followed her directions to her room but double-checked it was her sleeping in the bed before locking the door. Despite his exhaustion, his body hummed with anticipation as he undressed then slipped under the covers. She murmured in her sleep when he pulled her soft, warm body next to his.

It had only been a day since he'd lain with her yet he couldn't wait to feel her wrapped around his aching cock. He nuzzled her neck and ear then down to her collarbone.

She sighed dreamily then rolled to face him. With a gentle touch she traced his lips and cheek then slid her fingers into his hair. It wasn't clear who initiated it, but finally their lips met.

Within seconds their kiss went from a warm simmer to a full burn. All of the frustration he had built up during the day when he had been unable to touch her the way he wanted came unleashed. Needing to feel her skin upon his own, he pulled her nightgown up until he could slip his hand beneath.

She grasped his arm as if trying to get closer.

Unable to withstand the temptation, he rolled her onto her back then scooted down so he could feast upon her breasts. She kneaded her fingers in his hair as he licked and suckled one then the other.

When her hand wrapped around his erection he froze. That simplest of touches was very nearly his undoing. He groaned and pulled her hand away.

"Did I do something wrong?"

"No love."

"I just wanted to touch you."

"I know. Normally I would tell you to go ahead but I have been craving you all day. If you keep doing what you're doing then I won't last any time at all."

"Oh."

To stop any other questions she might have, he kissed her senseless. Her hand slid up his side and came to rest around his neck. Now that they were face to face again, he was able to pull one of her legs up and hook it over his hip. He slid his hand to the juncture between her legs and gloried in the fact that she was already wet for him. Keeping his lips upon hers, he muffled her sounds of pleasure as he worked her sensitive nub. When she began to rock against his hand he aimed his cock at her opening and eased his way inside. He kept his movements slow and steady despite his overwhelming need to drive into her body.

She moaned against his lips as she became lost in sensation. He slid one hand up her back to hold her firmly in place against his chest. The other he slipped between their bodies to find her nub again. It only took a few more flicks to send her careening over the edge. Her channel gripped him tightly and sent him spinning into oblivion also.

They remained locked in each other's arms until their breathing returned to normal. Then he slid out of bed to get a rag from the basin stand. He gently wiped her thighs then tossed the rag aside. Anxious to have her in his arms again, he slipped in next to her and pulled her firmly against him. No words were needed from either of them.

He fell asleep knowing he was exactly where he should be. They would talk about their future soon. Meanwhile, just being together was enough.

~ * ~

When dawn broke, Nathaniel smiled. He kissed Trixie on top of her head then slipped out of the bed. He dressed as silently as he could then made his way downstairs. He found Jacob in the kitchen enjoying a cup of coffee while watching out the back window.

"Good morning," Nathaniel said as he dropped his boots next to one of the unoccupied chairs.

Jacob raised a brow at his arrival. "You're an early riser."

"Afraid so." Nathaniel pulled his boots on. "Any disturbances last night?"

"None." Jacob took a sip from his cup. "Fletcher and I switched off somewhere around four this morning. If we get lucky we'll have a day to rest before those bastards come around again."

"They seem to want that journal pretty bad so I doubt we'll be that lucky."

Nathaniel helped himself to what was left of the coffee. Before he had a chance to finish Mrs. Ellison appeared.

She paused in the doorway of the kitchen as soon as she spotted Nathaniel. "Mr. Dennison. I didn't expect you until much later."

"Trixie is my priority. I wanted to be here as soon as I could to make sure she stayed safe."

Mrs. Ellison nodded. "Glad to hear it."

Nathaniel help up his cup. "I hope you don't mind that I helped myself."

"Not at all. I'll put on another pot in just a moment. I was about to begin breakfast for these gentlemen. You're welcome to join if you haven't eaten yet."

"I have not. I would appreciate it very much," Nathaniel smiled his gratitude.

She made shooing motions to the two of them. "Go make yourselves comfortable in the front room. I'll let you know when breakfast is ready."

"I think she's trying to get rid of us," Jacob said to Nathaniel.

"I believe so."

They grinned and left as directed. When they reached the foyer Jacob said, "Since you're here I think I'll take a quick pass around the block."

Nathaniel nodded then headed to the sitting room. He found three of the previous days' news sheets on the table. Since he didn't have the journal to work on, he settled in to read. He had just started reading the second in the stack when Trixie came in.

"Good morning, Mr. Dennison," she said from the doorway.

He tipped the corner down so he could see over the paper. "Good morning, Beatrix."

"Mrs. Ellison said you had arrived."

They shared a private grin as she joined him on the sofa. "She invited me for breakfast. I was making use of your recent news sheets while I waited."

"Anything of interest?"

"Nothing to keep my attention from you."

Mr. Ellison came to door. "The Missus said breakfast has been served in the dining room. You're welcome to help yourselves."

"Thank you, David," Trixie told the older man.

"Shall we?" Nathaniel said, getting to his feet. "I find myself famished this morning."

Trixie's cheeks turned pink. She put her hand in his and allowed him to escort her to the dining room. The smell of ham and fresh biscuits greeted them. Just as they sat, Jacob returned from his patrol.

"Notice anything while you were out?" Nathaniel asked.

"No." Jacob sounded faintly disappointed. "Strangely quiet area for London."

"That's one of the reasons Father always loved this house." She spooned a portion of porridge into a bowl then added a healthy splash of cream. "Most of the neighbors are older couples whose children have moved out. We've never noticed anyone coming or going at odd hours."

"That should make anyone who doesn't belong stand out."

"One would hope," Nathaniel muttered.

As they ate they chatted about one of the articles Nathaniel had read in the newssheets. He was about to enjoy his second helping of ham when something crashed in the kitchen. Mrs. Ellison screamed.

All three of them rushed from the dining room, Jacob in the lead. Nathaniel and Jacob both pulled weapons out as they ran. As soon as they burst into the kitchen they came to halt. On the other side of the room a man stood behind Mrs. Ellison with a gun pointed at her head. Mr. Ellison lay on the floor nearby. He had a gash on his forehead, but no injuries that appeared life threatening.

Mrs. Ellison's eyes were wide with fright as she glanced from them to her husband.

A second man came in through the back door. He pointed a pistol in their direction. "Go get the journal. Now."

Nathaniel stepped in front of Trixie. "What journal?" he asked.

"We don't have time for games. You know what journal we want. Get it now or this woman dies along with at least one of you."

Nathaniel quickly assessed the situation but didn't see a way out. Even if he managed to convince Trixie to get the journal and run out the front door - something she would never do when Mrs. Ellison was clearly in danger- the men would likely kill at least one of them and still chase after her.

Over his shoulder he told Trixie, "Go get the journal."

She nodded and hurried away.

Jacob and Nathaniel waited, still as two statues, and stared down their opponents. Even when Trixie returned, he didn't look away.

"Here. Just don't hurt her." Trixie tried to brush past but Nathaniel stopped her.

"No. You're not going near them." He plucked the journal

from her hand. "How shall we do this, gentlemen? You have pistols. We have pistols. You have something we want. We have something you want."

"Toss the book 'ere and we'll be on our way," the man holding Mrs. Ellison said.

"No."

"What do you mean no?"

"What guarantee do I have that you'll release her?" Nathaniel asked.

"You don't, mate," the second man said. "Seems to me we have a problem then."

"Well what do you think we should do, Goven'r?" the first man asked.

"How about if my friend," Nathaniel gestured to Jacob. "Brings you the book and he backs away with Mrs. Ellison?"

"Only if he comes without his pistol," the second man said.

Nathaniel and Jacob exchange glances. Jacob nodded then handed his pistol to Nathaniel in exchange for the journal. Jacob walked forward until he could reach Mrs. Ellison. He set the journal on the table near the men then pulled Mrs. Ellison behind him as soon as the man went for the book.

"Down!" Nathaniel ordered as he shoved Trixie backward, out of the kitchen. Jacob pushed Mrs. Ellison to the floor then Nathaniel opened fire on the men. The man fired back, grabbed the journal, then both men hurried out the door, slamming it closed behind them.

Nathaniel chased after the men but had to duck back into the house when the man fired another shot at him from further down the alley.

Jacob joined him at the door. "I'm going out the front."

"Here." Nathaniel handed Jacob's pistol back to him. "I'll follow them as soon as the alley is clear."

"Got it." Jacob hopped around the table and dashed out of the kitchen.

"Mrs. Ellison, are you all right?" Trixie asked from somewhere behind him.

Nathaniel didn't hear what Mrs. Ellison said. He tried to

remain focused on the sounds in the alleyway. A few people stuck their heads out but he waved them back inside their homes.

He startled when someone tugged at his jacket. "Dammit, Trixie! Get back inside and see to Mrs. Ellison."

"She said she's fine. She's tending Mr. Ellison. I'm coming with you."

"No, you're not." He looked back down the alley.

"Yes, I am."

"I don't have time to argue with you. I need to follow those men and try to get that journal back." He stepped out onto the walkway and darted in the direction the men had gone. When he heard her echoing footsteps behind him he said a prayer for strength. Why couldn't she come to her senses and stay at home where it was safe?

When he stopped at the edge of the next alleyway he grabbed her hand. "If you insist on coming, you have to do exactly what I tell you."

"That's always been a bit of a problem for me," she muttered.

22

"**DID** you see where he went?" Nathaniel pulled Trixie along behind him.

"No."

Their heads swiveled back and forth as they both searched the street and the alleyways they passed. They darted around the slower pedestrians and ducked out of the way of an oncoming horse and carriage.

"Dammit," Nathaniel swore under his breath. "I know he came this way. I'm certain of it."

"Where's the most likely place he would head?"

Nathaniel searched his memory banks. "Whitechapel, maybe. Or perhaps the market."

"What's down there?"

"People less likely to question your behavior."

"Hallo!"

Nathaniel and Trixie both looked toward the shout.

"Um… is that Willis?" Trixie asked.

"Yes." Nathaniel pulled her toward the edge of the road. He stopped only long enough to let a horse carrying a rider pass. "We're in a bit of a hurry. What are you doing here?"

"Carrick sent me to find you. He has a lead about where your brother went and wants you to meet him at the docks."

Nathaniel swore under his breath again.

"If Carrick is onto something, we might be better off finding him." She gestured to the crowded street. "We're not having any luck finding the men we were looking for. By now they could have handed the book off to any number of people who could have gone in any direction."

"True." He tipped his head to Willis. "Where can we find Carrick?"

Willis gave them directions to a seedy area down by the river. "Carrick said he'd join the two of you on the other side of the bridge but to act casual."

"I know the place," Nathaniel assured him. "Go back to Trixie's and get Fletcher and Jacob. We may need them."

"Will do." He gave Nathaniel a quick salute then turned toward her home.

Nathaniel led Trixie through the market and around to the bridge Willis mentioned. Once there he moved Trixie's hand onto his arm so they could stroll at a more leisurely pace. As soon as they crossed the footbridge Carrick moved in behind them. "We followed one of the men here late last night. He hired the ship over there on the left. It returned about an hour ago."

"What of the captain?"

"I followed him when he left the ship. He didn't go far. Took lunch at one of the local pubs then returned. He's still aboard. Samuel got close enough to see that he'd curled up in the cabin to sleep."

"What are you thinking is the best way to handle this then?"

"Captain looks like a regular. Nothing out of place about him or his ship. My guess is that he's just making extra money carting people back and forth for whoever is behind this. I'd take a direct approach. Offer him more money to take you to the same location. No questions asked."

"Seems reasonable." Nathaniel looked at Trixie. "I'm guessing you aren't going to let me take this boat ride alone, are you?"

"Not on your life."

"You do realize that it might be that risky, right?"

"Of course I do. But if there is a chance that my brother is wherever that man is going, I need to be there too."

Nathaniel sighed. "All right. Let's go."

"Wait." She tugged on Nathaniel's arm. "Don't we need a plan or something?"

Carrick shrugged. "We go in. Ask the Captain where he took his last passenger. If he answers we compensate him. If he doesn't we either offer him more coin or we find another way to convince him to answer us."

"Another way?"

The men glanced at each other but Trixie held up her hand. "I don't want to know. Just… just handle it." She brushed past them and headed to the ship.

Nathaniel caught her by the arm. "Let us do the talking when we get inside."

"I wouldn't dream of anything else."

Carrick snickered at Nathaniel's plight. When they reached the ship, he motioned for his men to join them. They discussed the plan then Carrick's men created a perimeter on the dock around the boat and one of the larger men in the group led the way onboard. The same man went inside the cabin and woke the Captain.

The man returned to the deck with a white haired, sea-weathered man who looked as if he'd been roused from his bed. "What devil are you doing on my boat?"

"You took a man out to sea last night at about half past midnight. Where did you take him?" Carrick said.

"Who wants to know?" the Captain asked.

"Doesn't matter," Nathaniel answered.

"Tell us where. We don't have much time," Carrick pressed.

The old captain leaned against the boathouse. He pulled a pipe out of his pocket and lit it. "What's in it for me if I tell you?"

"You could be saving a man's life. Isn't that worth something?" Trixie asked.

"Well, I don't know anything about a man's life being in danger. Anyone I've ever taken out on this here ship has been hale and hearty and willing to go where I took them."

Trixie crossed her arms over her chest and harrumphed.

"We have reason to believe that more than one person has

been taken against their will and one of those men is her brother. Will you help us find him?"

"I might be." He pointed his pipe at them. "For a price."

"And what is your price of passage?" Nathaniel asked.

The captain looked around him. "The whole lot of you wanting to go?"

"No. Only five of us." Carrick answered.

"One-way passage?"

Carrick and Nathaniel exchanged glances. Nathaniel answered, "That depends on the destination."

"What would you recommend, sir?" Trixie asked.

"Oh you'll be wanting round trip passage. The trick is knowing when you'll be returning."

"Is that something we can schedule?"

"That depends on your business there, now don't it?" the captain said.

"How much?" Nathaniel asked, cutting off the conversation.

"I'd say I could take the five of you out for ten shillings."

Carrick gave Nathaniel a brief nod.

"Each." The Captain quickly added.

"Wait a minute. You just—"

Nathaniel cut her off. "When can you be ready to leave?"

"Within the hour."

"Is your crew ready and able?"

"No crew. Just me and Jake."

"Jake?" Carrick asked.

He pointed to the lump of brown fur curled on a blanket in in the corner. "My dog."

Nathaniel nodded then looked to Trixie. "You don't get seasick, do you?"

"No. Never."

"And you can swim?"

"Of course."

Nathaniel nodded. "Very well. Within the hour," he told the captain.

"I'll be taking payment up front." The old man held out one

gnarled hand.

"We'll pay when we set sail."

The old man's eyes twinkled in amusement. "As you say." He went about readying the ship.

Nathaniel pulled Trixie along behind him. "Who do you want to send?" Nathaniel asked Carrick.

"I'll go. Samuel and Fletcher, too. Willis and Jacob can stay here and see if any more characters show up. After we see the destination I'll return with the Captain and make arrangements for reliable transport. Depending on what we find when we get there, Samuel and Fletcher can either stay with you two or return with me."

"Just what I was thinking," Nathaniel agreed.

"What about supplies?" Trixie asked.

"I'm afraid that we're winging it at this point," Nathaniel told her.

"Do you think I have time to send a note home?" she asked.

"I can send a message after I return." Carrick assured her.

"Mrs. Ellison will be worried," she explained.

"Understood." Carrick tipped his head toward his men. "Willis or Jacob can take a note while we're on the ship instead of waiting for my return."

"Thank you."

"Is there anything else you need?" Nathaniel asked her. "Perhaps a hat with a wider brim for while you're on the ship?"

"No, I'll be fine," she reassured him. "I'm used to being outside on the airships. I doubt it is much worse than long periods at sea."

Nathaniel nodded. "That's probably true."

"What about coin for the captain?" she asked.

"Between us we should have enough." Nathaniel raised a brow at Carrick. "But it wouldn't hurt to have a little extra."

Carrick looked past them toward the docks. "If you will excuse me I'll go and take care of that right now."

"What is he going to do?" Trixie asked Nathaniel.

"I suspect that he's about to relieve a few dice players out of some of their wages. He tipped his head toward a group of men gathered around a table behind one of the pubs.

23

THE captain navigated the ship next to a makeshift dock on an overgrown island. Because of the vine covered trees and dense underbrush it was hard to tell if the isle was inhabited or not.

"You left a man here?" Nathaniel asked.

The Captain took the pipe out of his mouth. "Yep."

Trixie scanned the forest ahead of them with in trepidation. When the boat stopped Nathaniel and Carrick lowered the gangplank then walked onto the boat ramp.

"Are you sure about this?" Carrick whispered.

"Don't see that we have any choice."

Carrick grimaced. "I'll return as soon as possible." He gestured to the trees. "And I'll bring supplies."

"Thank you." Nathaniel clasped hands with Carrick.

To Trixie, Carrick added. "Both of you take care."

"We will. Thank you for all of your help." She leaned up on her toes and placed a chaste kiss on Carrick's cheek.

He blinked in surprise and shuffled uncomfortably. But he also looked genuinely touched by the gesture.

"Captain." Nathaniel touched the brim of his hat.

"Thank you for bringing us," Trixie added.

"Good luck," the Captain said grimly.

Nathaniel waved Samuel and Fletcher ahead of them toward the trees. At least they had a somewhat worn path to follow. When they reached the edge of the trees, Nathaniel waved to Carrick, then followed Trixie and the others into the dense foliage.

As soon as he stepped into the forest, the sounds changed and the temperature dropped by several degrees. Without the hot sun beating down on them, the humid air became much more bearable.

Nathaniel checked the time on his pocket watch. There should be almost five hours of daylight left. They could probably cross the island in two if they kept a steady pace.

"Since we don't really know what we're looking for keep an eye out for treetop structures, caves, or clearings," Nathaniel told the others.

They hadn't made it far before Trixie remarked, "Does anyone else think it's strange that there are no signs of life?"

Samuel glanced over his shoulder at her. "Not really."

Fletcher stopped. "She's right."

The others came to a stop right behind him. Nathaniel frowned. She was right. Why hadn't he noticed that before?

Her head swiveled back and forth as she examined the tree tops. "I don't see or hear any birds or insects."

Fletcher shifted his pack further up on his shoulder. "We aren't that far out to sea. Shouldn't there be something living here?"

"You would think," Nathaniel muttered.

They all searched the trees above them.

"We need to keep moving," Nathaniel urged them onward.

Samuel nodded and resumed the lead. They walked another thirty meters then Samuel stopped.

"What's wrong?" Nathaniel asked from the rear.

"Oh my," Trixie's voice held a touch of awe.

Nathaniel moved closer and looked over Trixie's shoulder. The dense forested area had suddenly opened up. In the middle of the clearing someone had built a replica of an old stone castle from one of the English coastlines. It sat both perfectly and strangely out of place.

"How in the world..." Trixie's words trailed off as they all stared at the imposing structure before them. "Do you think Peter is in there?"

"I have no idea what to think."

"Should we go in?" she asked.

The men exchanged glances.

"Perhaps we should walk the perimeter to see what we might be dealing with here," Nathaniel suggested.

"Agreed," Fletcher said.

"Trixie and I will go this way." He pointed to the right. "The two of you take that direction. We'll meet in the middle on the other side of the castle."

"Got it." Samuel and Fletcher marched away.

"Come on," Nathaniel said to Trixie.

She nodded and followed him. "This is incredible. Who do you suppose built it?"

"Someone with a lot of money."

"But who has that kind of money?"

"Actually I could tell you several members of the ton who could afford it. But I can't think of any of them who would want to undertake such a thing."

"Do you think they have a dragon?" she asked.

"What?"

"A dragon. Do you think they have a dragon in the moat? Or somewhere on top of one of those towers? Maybe even a damsel in distress in one of the towers?"

He chuckled. "Let's hope not."

"Yeah. A dragon would be hard to beat."

They followed the rim of the forest to avoid being spotted by anyone in the castle. Despite the size of the castle, he didn't see people milling about. Strange.

When they made it more than half way around their side, Nathaniel altered their course a bit. He wanted a better look without alerting anyone or endangering Trixie. He weaved around the bushes and statues they found in a tended garden.

He had originally thought the windows to be leaded. Instead they had metal cages over them. Why would they need such security measures on a remote island?

At the primary opening of the structure sunlight glinted off what looked like dozens of statues. Closer inspection revealed the statues were moving. And they were moving in their direction.

"What is that?" Trixie asked.

"Nothing I want to find out about. Run!" He grabbed her hand and pulled her back into the garden. They darted and wove through the paths as he prayed they not been spotted.

His hopes were short lived. The ground vibrated with the sound of metal footsteps. The steps increased in speed and volume along with the sound of clicking gears.

"Nathaniel, look!"

Trixie's cry of alarm drew his attention. He swiveled to where she pointed. Through the row of bushes he could see a row of metal bodies, standing at attention.

"What are they?" Trixie asked.

"I have no idea."

He pulled her away from that side of the garden but soon more metal bodies blocked their way. He tried yet another path only to find it had been blocked as well.

"What do we do?"

"This way." He pulled her toward the castle. Perhaps they could run along the outside of the structure.

Another pair of the metal bodies blocked their way. Nathaniel pushed her behind him in an effort to shield her.

"Now what?" she asked.

The metal bodies lowered their spear like weapons at them, forcing them to back up. The metal men did not attack but continued to advance on them. When they had backed up as far as they could go, two more metal men appeared on the right.

They were surrounded.

"I think they want us to go into the castle," he told Trixie.

"I see that. But why?"

He shook his head. "I have no idea."

"Maybe those metal things are some kind of security?" she asked.

"Possibly."

They followed the metal men into the castle through the main entrance. Inside a massive stone staircase flowed up to the next level. Beautiful, yet imposing. A large metal chandelier hung overhead but wasn't needed due to the number of windows.

At the top of the stairs five men appeared. Real men. He recognized two. Thankfully neither were close acquaintances so he stood a chance of remaining unknown.

The grey headed man in the dark brown jacket stepped forward. "Good afternoon. What brings you to Candlewood?"

Not wanting Trixie to give anything away about their trip, Nathaniel said, "Good afternoon. We're searching for a friend of ours."

"Do you mean the two gentlemen we found in the south gardens?" the same man asked.

"Ah, no." Nathaniel smiled graciously. "But I am glad you found our companions."

"Do you realize you are trespassing?"

"I'm not surprised. But no, we didn't know that when we landed on the island. As I said, we came to find someone."

"What makes you think your friend is here?" The taller man in a dark suit asked.

"We have it from a reliable source that he boarded a ship that came this way. We thought this might be an abandoned island. Imagine our surprise when we found this beautiful estate in the middle of the sea."

"I'm sure," the tall man said.

"We have several guests in residence at this time," the gray-headed man said. "Perhaps your friend is one of them. What is his name?"

"Peter Wadeworth."

None of the men reacted to the name.

"And you are?" one of the men he recognized as Phineous Gilbralter asked.

He considered giving them a pseudonym, but the risk of being caught in a lie outweighed his need for secrecy given that two of them were familiar to him. Especially when one of the men he recognized was the Duke of Strathorn. "Nathaniel Dennison." His past connection to the Wadeworths justified his search for Peter without giving away his position with the RIO.

"And she is?" the gray headed man pointed to Trixie.

"My companion." Nathaniel said simply. "May I ask your name, sir?"

The man glanced at the Duke. "I'm Edwin Thompson. I oversee the estate when my lord is unavailable."

"And that would be Lord…" Nathaniel asked.

"Not your concern." Edwin gestured to the metal men. They moved closer to Nathaniel and Trixie. "You'll understand Mr. Dennison that we cannot have you wandering about the estate unattended. Until we can determine how to best accommodate you, we'll put you with your companions."

With that declaration, the five men turned and left the upper landing through a doorway behind them. Three human guards moved out the shadows.

One of the guards gestured to the hallway to their left. "If you'll follow me, Govern'r."

The three guards led them as well as a handful of metal men away from the front entrance. Much like Carrick's estate, their path took them through the kitchens, down a stone stairway, and through what appeared to be the wine cellar. They paused at a large wooden doorway while one of the guards unlocked it.

Dread filled Nathaniel but he maintained a calm appearance. Their accommodations would likely not be plush or comfortable.

The door creaked open. Cool, earthy air flowed around them. Odd. He had expected a damp musty smell. Perhaps even of decay and rot, as many underground areas did. Then again, the castle appeared to be recently built.

The metal men remained in place at the door while the human guards led the way down a set of curving stone stairs. When they reached the landing at the bottom they found two rows of metal cages in a brightly lit stone room.

Samuel and Fletcher got to their feet and moved to the door of their cells when they entered.

"We'll be taking your things now," one of the guards said.

Nathaniel slipped his shoulders from the straps of his pack and handed it over. He nodded to Trixie that she should do the same.

"Don't suppose you'd let me keep my book with me so I have something to read while we wait, will you?"

"No, Miss. Afraid that's not part of the deal. You see, a book could be used as a weapon."

Her brow furrowed and she looked to Nathaniel for confirmation.

He nodded and shrugged. "It's true."

She scowled at the guard as she slipped the strap of her bag over her head.

"Your pistol as well, mate." The other guard told him.

Nathaniel slowly upholstered his weapon so as to not alarm their captors. With Trixie standing in their midst, he didn't want to risk her getting caught in a scuffle. With the barrel end point downward, he handed it over.

"Anything else?" the guard asked.

Nathaniel pulled the knife strapped to his waist out and handed it to the guard also.

"Is that it?"

"Yes." It wasn't, but the small knife hidden in his vest and the one in his boot didn't need to be discussed.

"What about you, Miss? You carrying any weapons?"

Nathaniel held his breath.

"Only the one pistol," she told them.

The guard's brows rose expectantly.

"It's in the bag."

The guard scanned her from head to toe then gestured to his companion. That guard rummaged through her bag then nodded.

"Very well." The first guard gestured for them to proceed to the cells.

Nathaniel assessed their surroundings as well as Samuel and

Fletcher as they passed. While it was far more clean and well-lit than expected they were still in a dungeon.

"Are you two all right," Trixie asked Samuel and Fletcher.

"Surprisingly comfortable," Fletcher told her.

"Much cooler in here than out stomping around in a humid jungle."

"They even brought us fresh water," Samuel added with false cheer.

"Well good. I'm glad you've been taken care of." She lifted her nose at the guard. "I'm sure this misunderstanding will be cleared up shortly and we'll be on our way."

"Right. In you go, Miss," the guard said as he gestured to one of the empty cells.

Nathaniel attempted to follow her in but the guard stuck out his hand to stop him. "That one—" He gestured to the cell next to hers. "—is yours."

He exchanged glances with Trixie but moved toward the other cell. He waited until the guard shut and locked the door on Trixie's before entering his own. He wasn't about to leave her vulnerable to the guards if he could help it. So far they had acted with decorum, but he didn't trust that to remain.

The guard gestured for him to enter then shut the door behind him.

24

THE clang of the metal door echoed off the stone walls of their cell when the guard slammed it closed. At least the lock didn't crunch or grind when he turned the key as you might expect in a dungeon. Was it because the locks were new? Or because they were used so often they were well maintained? Neither possibility made her feel better.

Taking her cue from Nathaniel she maintained a calm outward appearance even though her heart hammered within her chest.

"How long do you plan to keep us here?" Nathaniel demanded from his cell.

"That's not up to me, Govern'r," the guard said as he and his companions walked away.

Nathaniel moved to the wall of metal bars separating the two of them. "Are you all right?" he asked Trixie.

"Mostly." She inspected their surroundings. "At least they didn't toss us into a dark hole."

"True." He went to the door of his cell. "Samuel. Fletcher. Are you well?"

"A few bumps but nothing to worry over," Fletcher answered.

The slam of door at the top of the stone stairway echoed through the room.

"I'm guessing neither of you figured a way out of here?" Nathaniel asked.

"Not yet," Fletcher told him.

Samuel added, "The locks are trickier than any I've seen. I'd need something to work with to even begin working it open."

Nathaniel inspected the door to his cell. "What about the hinges?"

"Solid construction. We'd need something for leverage to budge them," Samuel told him.

"We might be stuck until Carrick comes for us," Fletcher said.

"Or we just need the right tool." Trixie pulled Squeaks and Nid out of her pocket and set them on the ground next to the door. "See what you can do with those locks," she told her pets.

Squeaks ran up the bar to the lock on her cell and began to work the lock while Nid ran to Samuel's cell across from her.

Within seconds the tumblers in the lock lined up letting Trixie's cell door swing free. "Well done, Squeaks!" Trixie gathered her mechanical friend and hurried to Nathaniel's cell. "Can you open this one too?" She let Squeaks hop onto the bar.

Behind her, Samuel mumbled, "I'll be dammed."

"Take Nid to Fletcher's door so he can work on that lock," she said.

"These little guys are rather handy," Fletcher told her.

"Yes, they are." She smiled fondly.

The lock of Nathaniel's cell popped free. He swept Squeaks into the palm of his hand and yanked the door to his cell open. He went to Trixie and wrapped his arms around her. "Once again, your friends have served you well." He kissed the top of her head then held his hand out so that Squeaks could run onto her palm.

Fletcher's cell opened. Samuel and Fletcher joined them. "What's the plan?" Samuel asked.

"Get out of the dungeon. Find out if Peter is here," Nathaniel said.

Fletcher grunted. "No problem."

"How about if we start with the first part?" Trixie suggested.

"What did you two observe as you were brought in?" Nathaniel asked.

"One of those metal guards posted at the entrance. None inside. Either they don't have guards to spare or their over confident of the security of the dungeon."

"Were you brought in from the castle?"

"No." Samuel he pointed to a passage she hadn't noticed when they came in. "We came directly from the gardens. You didn't?"

"No. The metal guards escorted us through the front door. When the Duke ordered us to the dungeons, the guards took us through the kitchens and the cellar to get here."

"Was it well guarded?" Samuel asked.

"Not at all," Nathaniel told them.

"Then perhaps that would be the best way to return," Fletcher suggested.

"It's the castle we need to search, so I agree," Nathaniel said.

"Won't they miss us?" Trixie asked.

Fletcher shrugged. "Eventually."

"Then we won't have much time before they come looking for us," Trixie guessed.

"Maybe." Nathaniel told Samuel and Fletcher, "We should stay together this time." He gestured to Trixie. "She and I are the only ones who know what Peter looks like."

"Agreed," Samuel said.

Nathaniel led them to the passage that would take them to the cellars. When they reached the door he paused and listened. "The door is too thick to tell if there is anyone on the other side," he whispered.

"Can your spider thing tell us if the door is guarded?" Fletcher asked Trixie in a low voice.

"I don't see why not." She pulled Nid from her pocket and held him up to her face. "Nid, can you find your way to the other side and let us know if it's safe to pass?"

"And if the door is locked, could he unlock it?" Samuel asked hopefully.

"Yes. Unlock it too if you can," Trixie told them.

Nid shook one foot at her and bobbed its head. She set him on the ground next to the door. Nid attempted to pass under the door in several places along the bottom but didn't fit. Finally he squeezed through a gap at the corner.

Trixie held her breath and listened. Finally she heard faint scratching on the wood and a heavy thud. Then Nid wiggled his way back through the gap. She reached to pick him up. He sat up on his back legs and waved his front legs, gesturing to her and the door.

"It's safe to open the door now?" she asked.

Nid waved his legs then moved as if to run toward the door.

"What is he saying?" Nathaniel asked.

"I think it's safe."

"I'll try it," Samuel offered.

"Stay back, just in case." Nathaniel gestured for her to back away from the door.

She clutched Nid against her chest and pressed her back against the wall. Her heartbeat sped up as she waited for Samuel to open the door.

He stuck his head through the opening then gestured for them to follow.

She let out the breath she didn't realize she had been holding and followed Nathaniel and Fletcher. Nathaniel took her hand and pulled her along behind him. "This way," he told Samuel and Fletcher.

They moved swiftly and quietly through the kitchen storage. Only stopping long enough to hide when someone passed through an adjacent archway.

Nathaniel led them to a large open hallway. Since they found no one in that wing they made their way down the hall, checking each doorway as they passed.

"Did everyone leave?" she asked.

"I doubt it," Nathaniel said. "It's more likely that there aren't many people here." He took her hand again. "We'll keep looking."

Once again Samuel led the way and attempted to open the

massive door at the end. "It's locked."

"Where do you suppose it leads?" Fletcher asked.

"Based on its proximity to the kitchens and the front entrance my guess would be a ballroom," Nathaniel told them.

"Why would they need a ballroom?" Trixie asked.

"I can't even begin to guess." Nathaniel pointed to the kitchens. "If this is the ballroom it likely takes up the rest of this wing. We should be able to make our way to the next wing without going outside."

"Works for me," Samuel said.

"Trixie, would you ask one of your pets to handle the lock?" Nathaniel asked.

"Of course." She reached into her pocket and pulled out Squeaks. "Should I have Nid see if it's safe to open the door?"

"Certainly can't hurt."

She set her pets down next to the door. Nid squeezed under while Squeaks went to work on the lock. Once again Squeaks opened the lock with ease.

"Nid hasn't returned. Should we go ahead do you think?" Trixie asked the men.

"We can't stay here. I say we keep moving," Samuel said.

"Agreed. Someone's bound to come along eventually," Fletcher added.

Nathaniel nodded. "I'll take the lead this time. You two cover the rear."

"Got it," Fletcher said.

"Trixie, get behind me."

She pocketed Squeaks then moved in behind Nathaniel.

Nathaniel eased the door open a fraction then peeked through the narrow gap. "What the devil?" he murmured.

"What do you see?" she whispered.

"It appears to be some kind of workroom." He opened the door wider.

Nid scurried across her boot. She scooped him up then peeked around Nathaniel's shoulder. Sunlight streamed in through the large curtain-less windows that lined the walls to their left and straight ahead. She had expected to find an empty ballroom. Possibly a couple of guards stationed at adjoining doors. Instead the room was full of parts, worktables, and metal stands.

Nathaniel moved farther into the space, letting her, Samuel and Fletcher enter behind him.

"What do you suppose…" Trixie's question died on her lips when she spotted rows of the metal guards in various states of completion grouped in one corner.

"So they make those things here?" Samuel asked softly.

"Apparently so." Nathaniel pulled the door closed behind them.

Trixie searched the room for signs of life. "But who is making them?"

One of the doors to their right opened.

Nathaniel grabbed her hand and pulled her down beside him as he squatted behind a barrel. Samuel and Fletcher dove for cover behind nearby tables.

Whoever came in went to one of the tables and began moving things around.

Nathaniel looked over at Samuel and Fletcher. Samuel gestured to him. Trixie took his hand motions to mean that they would move in and knock out whoever had come in. She grimaced and peered around the barrel to see how far way their victim was.

The man stood with his back to them. He wore a dirty, white shirt and dark trousers. His head was bent over whatever he worked on making it hard to tell how old he was. Based on the size and shape of his shoulders she guessed he was about the same age as Nathaniel.

When the man turned to grab something from a nearby table she got a look at the profile of his face. She gasped and jumped to her feet. "Peter!"

25

NATHANIEL tried to grab Trixie's hand when she jumped, but hesitated because of her exclamation. He scrambled to his feet to follow.

"Trixie." Peter dropped whatever he had been holding. It landed with a resounding clang. "What the devil are you doing here?" He rushed toward Trixie.

Nathaniel quelled his impulse to pull her back.

"Peter, are you all right?" Trixie threw her arms around Peter, oblivious to the dirt and grime that coated his clothes and apron. "I've been so worried about you."

"I'm fine. How did you get here?" He looked in Nathaniel's direction. "Nathaniel." Peter grinned then frowned. "You guys can't be here. It's not safe."

"We're here to rescue you," Trixie told him.

Peter shook his head. "You can't. There's no way off this island that the Duke doesn't control." He glanced at Nathaniel with a grimace. "Believe me, I've tried."

Nathaniel drew up beside Trixie. "What's going on here?"

Peter shook his head. "Nothing you want to know about. There's no time. I don't know how you got here but you have to get her out of here. If he finds out she's here—"

"Who?" she demanded.

"The Duke. He owns this island and everything on it. If he finds her, he'll use her, too."

Nathaniel scowled. "Use her for what?"

"For leverage." Peter hurried to one of the windows and

looked out.

"Leverage for what?" she asked.

Peter went to one of the windows on the other wall. "To make us do what we don't want to do."

She chased after him. "Such as?"

The last piece of the puzzle fell into place. "He's making you build his metal men, isn't he?" Nathaniel asked.

Peter's expression was grim. "Yes."

"Whatever for?" Trixie asked.

"Doesn't matter. You need to go. Now," Peter told her.

"No!" She jerked her arm from Peter's grip. "I'm not going anywhere without you."

"You have to." Peter swiped one hand across his face. "You don't know what he's like." He pleaded with Nathaniel. "Please. Get her out of here."

Nathaniel pulled Trixie back. She fought his grip. "I will. But tell me what we're dealing with first. I can't protect her if I don't know what we're up against."

Peter gestured to the metal men. "He's building an army. We're all trying to stop him, but he is holding something over each of us."

"Who is us?" Nathaniel pressed.

Peter's frustration came through in his words and gestures. "I'm not sure who everyone is. For the most part he keeps us separated. I've worked with Dr. Brewer and Carlin James a time or two since I've been here. And I've managed to exchange notes with Henry Hayward."

"The missing scientists," Nathaniel said.

"Someone finally realized they were missing?" Peter asked with a touch of attitude.

"The RIO has been investigating disappearances for months." Nathaniel told him. "We simply had nothing to go on. No witnesses or evidence to support kidnapping, murder, or abandonment." He shook his head. "Nothing." He pointed at Peter. "Until you."

Peter frowned. "What did they leave behind when they took me?"

"Her." Nathaniel gestured to Trixie. "She knew something had happened to you and she wasn't about to give up until she found you."

Peter shook his head. "Dammit Trixie." His expression of worry turned into one of fondness. "I should have known you'd come looking for me. I just wish you hadn't."

Trixie's eyes filled with tears. "Peter."

Her pain-filled voice made Nathaniel's chest ache. "How do we get back to the dock?"

Peter switched his attention back to Nathaniel. "I'm not certain. I have only made the trip once but I don't recall it being hidden." He picked up a pencil and rummaged around on the desk until he found a piece of paper. "Getting to the dock isn't the biggest issue. Once you get there, you'll need some kind of boat or ship to get back to London."

"We have one coming," Nathaniel assured him.

"Good." Peter tipped his head toward Trixie. "Then get her out of here."

Trixie reached for Peter. "You're coming with us, right?"

Peter took a step back. "I can't."

Trixie took another step. "Why not?"

"Because," Peter said, then glanced at Nathaniel before swinging his attention back to Trixie. "There are things you don't know."

"Seems there are many things we do not know." Samuel said as he and Fletcher advanced on Peter. "Perhaps you should enlighten us."

"I can't." Peter took a step back then stopped and lifted his chin. He looked directly at Trixie. "I can't."

"No. He really can't." A man said from somewhere above them.

Everyone turned to see who had spoken. The Duke stood on the dais, overlooking the ballroom. Two metal men flanked him on each side and one of the guards who had escorted them to the dungeon lingered behind.

The doors of the ballroom burst open. Metal men filled the openings, blocking their escape.

Nathaniel's gut filled with dread. They were surrounded.

"Who is that?" Trixie whispered.

"That is the man you have to worry about," Peter told her.

"I'm afraid that Peter's services are required for a bit longer my dear," the Duke said.

"For what?" she asked.

The Duke gestured to the whole ballroom. "For this of course."

"What? This mess?" she asked, almost mocking him.

"No, child. My creations," the Duke said with obvious pride.

"Your creations?" she challenged him. "You mean these chunks of walking metal?"

"Trixie," Nathaniel cautioned her.

The Duke scowled at her.

"Why do I have a feeling that you had very little to do with the actual creation of anything here? You're probably just another one of those old men with little skill and even less morals who want to be remembered for something great so you leverage the only thing you have. Your money. Then you ride on the back of those you see as your lesser by buying a few supplies and take credit for all of their hard work."

As she spoke she moved toward the Duke. Peter moved to another workbench and slipped something into his pocket.

"You have a sharp tongue my dear. You should take care with whom you choose to wield it upon."

"Truth hurts doesn't it?" she pressed.

"So, too, does a blade." The Duke gestured to someone outside the dais. "As I was saying, Peter is going nowhere. He has work to complete."

"And what if he doesn't want to stay?" she asked.

"He and I have an understanding."

"You and I do not however," Nathaniel said, drawing the Duke's attention. "I assume we are free to leave."

"You, sir, trespassed on my land."

"Unknowingly," Nathaniel countered.

"Trespassers, nonetheless, must be dealt with accordingly."

"You realize, of course, that people know where we were heading and why," Nathaniel reminded the Duke. "We will be missed if we're gone for long."

"Perhaps." He pointed at Trixie. "I have use for her, but you and your friends, I do not."

"I am a useful sort, what about you, Fletcher?" Samuel said.

"Me mum always did say I could be useful when I put my mind to it," Fletcher said.

"I thought you were both quite helpful the last few days," Nathaniel added.

"Silence!" the Duke roared. "Quincy, take her to the tower and lock her away. Return the others to the dungeons until I can decide what to do with them."

The guard who had been hovering near the door of the dais left, presumably to come and fetch her.

"No!" Trixie ran to Nathaniel and during a dramatic display of affection slipped Squeaks into his pocket. "I'm not going anywhere without him."

"Your concern for this man does not move me in the least. I can assure you that your accommodations in the tower will be much more comfortable than those of the dungeon."

"I thought your dungeon was by far the nicest I have ever been in," Samuel said.

Fletcher nodded. "I agree."

"Much better than those at Grendola," Samuel added.

"Oh, definitely," Fletcher said. "Probably because it doesn't have a river of trash running through it."

If he hadn't been so worried about Trixie, Nathaniel might have laughed at their antics. He just prayed that they had been able to hold enough of the Duke's attention away from Peter. He strongly suspected Peter was up to something.

Quincy, the guard, came through one of the doors and headed in their direction.

"No!" Trixie cried out.

Nathaniel stepped between her and Quincy.

Quincy stopped when Samuel and Fletcher took up places next to her. He glanced at the Duke then gestured for her to come forward.

Trixie shook her head and tightened her grip on his jacket. "No." She looked up at the Duke. "I told you I'm not going anywhere without Nathaniel. I'd rather go to the dungeons with them."

"Why must you make this difficult?" The Duke motioned to someone near the dais. "Bring him."

Peter circled around the table next to them. "Trixie, I know you don't understand what's going on. I'm sure you're scared and want to make sure your friends are safe. I mean…" He glanced up at the Duke. "After all, they did help you come all this way."

"Y-yes," she nodded at Peter.

"But sometimes we have to do things that we don't want to do, for the good of other people."

What was Peter up to? His behavior was making him uneasy.

"Enough of this. Take the girl," the Duke ordered.

Quincy moved in and attempted to grab Trixie's arm. She shook off his grip. Nathaniel punched Quincy in the side of the head.

The metal men in the doorway moved in behind Quincy.

Samuel and Fletcher grabbed pieces of metal from the tables to use as weapons. Trixie snatched a metal pipe.

"Trixie don't do this. They're programmed to respond to violence," Peter cautioned. "If you attack, they will counter attack."

"That's right, child. I suggest that you listen to your brother and go with Quincy peacefully. That's the only way to ensure your friends aren't killed on the spot."

Trixie looked at Nathaniel.

He assessed the situation. Metal men outnumbered them. The metal men's abilities were unknown. Peter appeared to be cooperating with the Duke for unknown reasons. The dungeons were not unsafe. He had the means to escape again since Trixie passed Squeaks to him. Trixie would be taken someplace that might be more comfortable for her but her safety questionable. Peter seemed unconcerned about her safety. Peter's mental state was questionable.

Dammit. There were too many unknowns for his liking. His gut screamed that he should follow Peter's lead but he just couldn't let them take Trixie someplace he couldn't protect her.

"Your time is up." The Duke declared. "Put down the weapons and surrender or your friends will be shot where they stand."

"No!" Trixie yelled.

"Beatrix Madeline Wadeworth, put that down before you get hurt," a man said from one of the ballroom doors.

Trixie gasped and whipped around.

Nathaniel reached to steady her when she swayed unsteadily.

The metal pipe she held clattered on the floor. "Father?"

26

TRIXIE blinked back the tears that had pooled in her eyes. Even though there had been hints that he was alive she still couldn't believe it.

"Father? Is it really you?" Her voice cracked.

Thomas Wadeworth smiled and moved further into the room. "It is."

Her head swam and her feet drug across the floor as if she were slogging through ankle-deep mud. As soon as she was within arm's reach she launched herself into his arms.

He hugged her tightly against his chest and whispered into her ear. "It's all right little bumble bee. It will be fine." He lowered his voice where only she could hear him. "Listen to Peter and do what he says."

She lifted her head and gave him a quick nod. "You look exactly as I remember." Her eyes darted to his hair and she gave him a watery smile. "But maybe with a little more gray hair."

He smiled down at her. "That happens as you get older, my dear." He glanced up at the Duke. "One day you'll see."

"Yes, let's all hope so." The Duke leaned on the banister. "Well this has been a touching reunion, but we have business to take care of and deadlines to meet. Quincy, if you please?"

"No." Thomas said as he herded her closer to Peter and Nathaniel. "You promised if I helped you that my children would never be harmed. Yet here they are."

"And they're unharmed, aren't they?" the Duke countered.

"Let her go," Thomas insisted.

"Afraid I cannot do that. She knows too much." The Duke gestured to Nathaniel, Samuel, and Fletcher. "They all do. No one leaves this island until I have my army."

"That wasn't part of the agreement," Thomas said.

"She changed the terms of the agreement by coming here. I didn't bring her here," the Duke declared.

"No, but I would wager it was you who sent me and Peter the threatening letters wasn't it?" Trixie said.

"What letters?" Thomas asked.

"Letters demanding we locate and deliver your journal," Peter admitted. "They came not long before they grabbed me."

Thomas shot the Duke a withering look.

"I suspect that's when he discovered I had continued your research for an alternative power source," Peter added.

"Which is why you changed your plans. If you couldn't have the diary, then perhaps a father-son team might solve your little problem. Is that right?" Thomas asked.

"Why not have both?" The Duke held up the diary.

Peter and her father both cringed.

The Duke chuckled. "So you see, I don't really need either of you."

Nathaniel spoke up. "Actually, I'm afraid you still do. Perhaps you've already discovered that the book is very nearly impenetrable. And even if you do manage to break through the casing you'll find that the text is coded." He tipped his head at Thomas, in a sort of salute. "A well thought out code too, I might point out."

"Oh, and what do you know about these things?" the Duke sneered.

"Actually code work is my specialty," Nathaniel admitted.

The Duke lifted his chin.

"As a member of the Royal Intelligence Office."

Even from where they stood, she could see that the Duke's face had turned red.

"Guards," the Duke bellowed. "Take them! Secure the castle and send men out to the dock. Prepare for unwanted company immediately." The Duke turned to exit the dais.

The metal men advanced further into the room. Their heavy footsteps echoing through the room like gunshots.

Quincy stepped back, giving them room. Samuel and Fletcher prepared to defend themselves.

Trixie's heartbeat sped up. She grasped her father's jacket and edged away from the metal men.

"A moment more, your lordship," Peter called out.

The Duke stopped and shot him a haughty look of annoyance.

The metal men moved closer, one heavy step at a time.

"I am afraid your army may not meet all of your requirements," Peter said.

Trixie and Nathaniel exchanged glances.

The Duke returned to the banister. "What do you mean?" Pounding footsteps very nearly drowned out his question.

"One of your specifications was that they respond to all of your voice commands."

"And that was met," the Duke waved to the advancing army.

"With one exception," Peter said.

The Duke tightened his grip on the bannister. "And what would that be?"

"When I override your commands." Peter used his thumb to push the button on the device he held.

The metal men stopped their advance. Each one of them slumped forward. Their metal arms and heads hung loosely from their bodies.

"Grab that device," the Duke ordered.

Quincy leapt toward Peter but Samuel and Fletcher blocked his way. Two more human guards entered but hesitated just inside the door.

"The device will do you no good, actually," Peter told the Duke.

"It's a fail-safe we added to ensure your army couldn't be used against us or any other human," Thomas added.

"You." The Duke pointed at Peter and Thomas. "You will

pay for this deception." He turned and stomped off of the dais through the open doorway.

"We need to stop him," Peter told Nathaniel as they engaged the two guards who had joined the fray. "He has grand plans of marching into London and unseating the Queen."

"That's what he wanted an army for?" Trixie asked as she kept watch from behind.

"Yes," Thomas confirmed.

"He's mad," she said.

Samuel and Fletcher subdued Quincy then Samuel went to assist Nathaniel and Peter.

"Here." Trixie tossed Fletcher a length of rope she found on one of the workbenches.

"Thanks." Fletcher flipped the unconscious Quincy over and bound his hands behind his back.

"Peter. Your mother," Thomas said.

Peter kicked the man closest to him in the stomach then elbowed him in the back of his head. "You have him?" Peter asked Nathaniel.

"Yes." Nathaniel restrained the man. Peter skirted around them and ran out of the ballroom.

Samuel knocked out the man he had been fighting with and came to assist Nathaniel.

Nathaniel jerked his head to Peter's retreating back. "Go with him."

"Got it." Samuel ran after Peter.

Trixie froze. "What about mother?" she asked her father.

Thomas stopped his rummaging through parts and drawers. "You mother is alive. The Duke took us both. She's here in the castle."

Trixie slumped against a nearby table. "She's alive?"

Thomas grabbed her by the arms. "Yes. It's how the Duke has been controlling me. He uses her and the two of you as pawns in his sick game to ensure I get a proper amount of work done on his machines."

"But you've been gone for more than five years."

"I know." He squeezed her arms. "Believe me. I know. And

if there had been any way of getting word to the two of you, I would have." He kissed her on top of her head. "But there's no time for that right now. We need to find as many of the diagrams for these machines as we can. They need to be destroyed before they can be used by someone even worse than the Duke."

Trixie snapped out of her shock and went to a nearby table. She rummaged through the various parts scattered across the top. "Where would they be?" She opened a couple of the drawers to check inside.

"They could be anywhere. The Duke wouldn't allow us to collaborate very often. And lately Peter has carried the bulk of the work load alone." He held up a piece of paper with scribbled words and pictures. "Just grab anything that looks like instructions."

"Got it."

"Where did you find that rope?" Fletcher yelled from across the room.

"On that table," she pointed out the one she meant.

"Uh… a little help would be appreciated," Nathaniel said.

"Go ahead," Thomas told her. "Help them."

She nodded then fetched the rope.

As Nathaniel and Fletcher secured the two guards an explosion shook the castle.

"What was that?" Fletcher asked.

Nathaniel's brow furrowed with concern.

"Eva," Thomas murmured. He dropped the papers he had been collecting and headed to one of the ballroom doors.

Nathaniel cut him off. "Wait. You cannot just run off on your own, sir. We don't know how many more guards the Duke has. Nor do we know what that explosion was."

"Move aside. I need to get to Eva."

"Peter went to get her, correct?" Nathaniel asked him.

"Yes." Thomas tried to step around Nathaniel but was blocked again.

"Then let him do his job."

"But—"

"If you go chasing after them, you could end up passing them by way of a different corridor then we'll be scattered all over the castle." Nathaniel blocked his attempt to pass again. "Trust Peter to do what he has to. Samuel went with him. They will find your wife, sir. I'm certain of it."

The muscle in Thomas' jaw flexed but he finally relented with a nod of his head.

Nathaniel gestured to the workspace. "Now that we have these men secured, what can we help you with?"

"We need to search everything for notes or diagrams that show how to build these things," he pointed to one of the partial built metal men.

"We've already searched these tables here." Trixie pointed to the handful they had collected.

"Just grab anything you find, even if it looks insignificant. Most of the plans were broken into small sections to make it harder for anyone to piece the whole picture together."

"Smart," Nathaniel said.

Between the four of them, they managed to search most of the workspaces before they were interrupted again.

"Thomas!" A woman exclaimed from the doorway. "Bea!"

Trixie's heart tripped over itself. She ran to the woman she never thought she would see again. "Mother!"

Thomas dropped the box he had been sorting through and followed Trixie to the door.

"Oh, my darling girl." Evaline Wadeworth wrapped Trixie in her arms. Tears flowed from both women as they murmured nonsensical greetings to each other.

When they had gotten over most of their blubbering, Thomas joined them. With an arm around each of them, he kissed Trixie on top of her head and then on Eva's cheek.

"Peter found you well, wife?"

"He did." She looked over her shoulder and motioned for Peter to join their group.

Peter only hesitated a second before he did.

"I'm afraid I need to cut this reunion short," Nathaniel told them. "We still don't know where the Duke went and we need to get everyone out of here."

Eva and Trixie wiped their eyes.

Thomas cleared his throat. "The castle needs to be searched for the other scientists, but my priority is getting Eva and Trixie off this island. Preferably under guard."

"I'm not going anywhere without the rest of you," Trixie said.

"Nor am I," Eva added.

"Eva please," Thomas pleaded.

"Thomas. I've been trapped on this island with you for the last five years. If you think I am about to abandon you now, you've lost what little sense you have left. Do not ask it of me."

"We will all be leaving this island," Nathaniel assured them. "What needs to happen right now is to ensure everyone brought here against their will are safe."

"Agreed," Peter said. "You said you had people coming?"

"Yes. Unfortunately, I don't know when, but I expect sometime soon." Nathaniel smirked. "Carrick wouldn't want to miss a fight."

"There's movement out front," Samuel called from one of the windows.

Nathaniel and Peter joined him at the window. Thomas held Eva and Trixie back.

"Speak of the devil," Nathaniel said. He told Trixie over her shoulder, "It's Carrick and his men."

"Looks like they had a run in with the Duke." Samuel told them. "I believe that might be his lordship tied behind the wagon."

Peter chuckled. "And he looks rather unhappy about his current predicament."

"I'll meet him at the front entrance," Nathaniel said.

"Does that mean we're really free?" Eva asked Thomas.

"I believe so, my dear." Thomas wrapped an arm around Eva and kissed her on top of the head.

Trixie's heart soared. She moved to her mother's other side and wrapped her arm around Eva's waist. With a sigh of contentment, Trixie lay her head against her mother's shoulder.

27

TRIXIE sat at her desk, pen in hand, watching a bird hop from branch to branch in the tree just outside her parent's sitting room window. For no less than the tenth time that morning she wondered what Nathaniel was doing and when he would return to London. Her list of things to tell him had grown too long to remember. She was also anxious to know that he was still hale and unharmed.

She grew warm. And in truth, she longed to be able to curl up next to him during the night and to feel his arms wrapped around her.

"Did you finish those invitations yet?" her mother asked.

"What?" She glanced at the envelopes still stacked neatly where they had been when she started. "Oh. No, I didn't…"

Eva put a hand on her shoulder. "Are you all right, dear?"

"Yes. I'm fine."

Her mother raised one brow.

"No. I'm not." She let the pen fall from her fingers and dropped her head into her hands.

"Do you want to talk about it?"

"No." She moaned. Then looked up at her mother. She still couldn't believe she was here. "Yes." She grabbed her mother's hand. "I don't know what to do."

"About what?" Her mother pulled the nearby stool closer and sat. "Surely you're not worried about the Duke."

"No." Trixie waved that thought away with the flick of her wrist. "I don't know what to think about Nathaniel."

"What about him?"

"Other than the one note to say his superior had ordered him to remain on the island until the investigation was complete, he hasn't written or come home or anything."

"Isn't he working, dear?"

"Yes," she moped.

"I'm sure he'll be in contact as soon as he can."

"Do you really think he will?"

"After everything the two of you went through together? I most certainly do." She patted Trixie's knee. "Besides, he said he would, didn't he?"

"Yes. But…"

"But what?"

"But then what?" Trixie whispered.

"What do you mean?"

"What happens when he returns?"

"What do you want to happen?"

"I…" She blinked. Her mouth hung open but words failed to form. Her heart sped up.

"You care for him, don't you?" her mother asked.

A knot formed in her throat. She had to choke it down before she could answer. "Very much."

Her mother reached for her hand. "Then make sure he knows."

"But what if he doesn't feel the same for me?"

Her mother lifted one shoulder and let it fall. "What if he does and you never say anything and he never says anything and the two of you miss out on an opportunity to have a beautiful life together?" She smiled. "I think that would be a far worse thing."

Trixie lifted her chin. "You're right. I can do it."

She stood. "After all, I've flown an airship. And handled bankers and dockworkers. I can tell a man how I feel. And even if he rejects me, I'll be just fine."

"If who rejects you?" Peter asked from the doorway.

"No one," Trixie and her mother said at the same time.

Peter frowned. "Well, when you're done plotting against the

172

menfolk of this town, would you mind posting these letters when you go out this afternoon?"

"Yes. Certainly." Trixie took the envelopes from Peter.

He shot a strange look at their mother then walked away shaking his head.

"Now about those invitations," her mother said. "Perhaps we can work on this stack together?"

Trixie went back to her desk. "I promise to focus this time."

No sooner had they settled in to address the envelopes when the bell at the front door rang.

Franklin, her father's recently acquired man, greeted whoever was at the door. Peter's muted voice floated through the open doorway. Trixie tried to not listen but she was curious about who would be dropping by so early in the morning. Immediately after, her father joined Peter and the visitor in the foyer.

Their voices faded as they had retreated to her father's office across the hall.

Probably another of her father's old colleagues coming to call after hearing the news that he'd miraculously returned from the dead, with accolades from the Queen for services to the crown, no less.

She snorted to herself. Amazing how a little thing like a nod from the King brought the ton to your side in droves.

Sometime later – exactly seven envelopes worth – her father appeared in the doorway. "Eva, would you mind assisting me?"

"Certainly, dear." Her mother gave the envelope she had been addressing one last flourish then set the pen on the desk.

Trixie watched with a mixture of awe and a tiny bit of jealousy at the way her mother and father gazed at each other. Like there was no one they would rather see. Maybe one day she would be so lucky.

She snorted. And hopefully it wouldn't require them being taken prisoner by a crazy person to appreciate their feelings for each other.

"Trixie, do you have a minute?" Peter asked from the door.

"Do you have another errand for me to run this

afternoon?" Now that her father had returned along with Peter, there wasn't as much at Panhurst Air that needed her attention. She had taken to running errands for her parents as well as Peter to try and stay busy.

She gratefully set her pen aside.

"No, nothing like that. I just wanted to make sure you were free." He looked over his shoulder. "There's someone who wants to speak to you."

"To me?" She turned in her seat. "Whoever would—" The words died on her lips when Nathaniel appeared behind Peter. She quickly got to her feet. "Nathaniel. What are you—" She tucked a strand of hair behind her ear. "I mean, when did you return to London?"

Nathaniel stepped around Peter. "Late last night."

"I, uh—" Peter pointed to the back of the house. "I need to check on my carriage. Excuse me." He quickly disappeared around the corner.

Trixie frowned.

"May I?" Nathaniel asked, gesturing to the sofa.

"Yes. Do have a seat."

"Thank you," he murmured. He sat the package he carried on the table in front of him.

She sat in the chair she had been using. "How are you?"

"I'm well. How are you?"

"I am well also, thank you." She straightened an imaginary line in her gown. He seemed nervous. What would he have to be nervous about? Perhaps he had news of the Duke. "Is everything finished on the island?"

"No. Not yet."

Her hope that he might be home for good faded.

"But a couple of the other RIO officers have been assigned to finish collecting evidence. I have everything I need to file my report."

"Do they still think they will be able to get a ruling against him?"

He shrugged. "His family has a lot of money and connections so it's hard to say. I know I've done my part to the best of my ability. And the Queen is now aware of his plans. So even if his family manages to set him free, he'll be forced to leave the country."

"Good." She tapped the desk with her finger. "Although, I for one, hope he sees the noose."

"With good reason."

"What about the other families?" she asked.

"They've all been reunited. Some of them better than others. But at least everyone has been freed." He shuffled his feet. "The most amazing part of it all is that other than Mr. Silverton and four of the Duke's hired men, no one was killed."

"Mr. Silverton was the older scientist who died while in captivity, correct?"

"That's right. But even your father said it wasn't due to poor treatment." Nathaniel shrugged. "Although the pressure from the Duke's deadlines may have contributed."

"How could one man affect so many lives and not feel any guilt over it?"

Nathaniel shook his head. "I have no idea."

They fell silent for a moment.

"I brought you a gift." Nathaniel gestured to the package.

"What is it?" she asked.

"Open it and see."

She moved to the sofa. He made room for her to sit next to him. She plucked at the string on the box and untied it. As soon as she lifted the lid the smell of butter and chocolate tickled her senses. She closed her eyes and inhaled deeply. "Are those Mr. Henderson's?"

"Of course." He grinned. "I had rather hoped to arrive before mid-morning tea so I could share those with you."

Without even looking inside she set the box back on the table. "I'll ask Mrs. Ellison to bring us a tray."

She hopped up and practically skipped to the kitchen. When she returned she found Nathaniel staring out the window. His hands were clasped behind his back and he appeared to be deep in thought.

She stood in the doorway for a moment and drank in the

sight of him.

His jacket fit across his shoulders just perfectly. His hair had just started to curl at the back of his neck. Probably due to his unexpected stay on the island. But she rather liked the look of it. In truth, she liked the look of everything about him.

He turned toward her, startling her out of her thoughts. "Tea will be here in a moment." She joined him at the window.

"I assume your parents return has gone well?" he asked.

"Yes. It seems London is all aflutter with the news of their return from the dead." She chanced a glance up at him. "Of course recognition from the Queen sped that along."

He tipped his head. "I'm sure it did."

"I suppose we have you to thank for that?"

"Actually, that was Carrick's doing. He has the Prince's ear, you know."

"No, actually, I didn't. I suppose I shall have to send him a letter thanking him."

He glanced at her. "Thank him for what? Excessive social calls?" He snorted. "Hardly. Carrick hates them more than I."

"Still, it made their transition back into society much smoother. And it overrode all of those horrible accusations about father's disappearance." She touched his arm. "I can't thank him enough for that alone."

He put his hand over hers. "Carrick has been on the receiving end of the ton's displeasure more than once. Believe me when I say he understands just how fickle the ton can be. It's why we both avoid it like the plague."

They stood side by side at the window until Mrs. Ellison arrived with the tea tray. "Here we go," she said brightly as she breezed into the room. She set it on the table. "Can I bring you anything to go with the tea?"

"No, thank you, Mrs. Ellison. The tea is enough." Trixie said as she sat on the edge of the couch.

Mrs. Ellison smiled at Nathaniel then returned to the kitchens.

"Shall I pour?" she asked Nathaniel.

"Please."

Her heart flipped in her chest when he sat beside her instead of in the chair across from her. She poured for both of them then gestured to the box. "Would you care for one?"

His lips twitched. "Of course."

"Well you never know. You might have—" She stared down into the box, unsure of what she was seeing. In the middle of the box, surrounded by a half dozen pastries, sat a small jeweler's box. She glanced at Nathaniel in confusion.

"Go ahead," he encouraged her. "Open it."

She took the small box out then set the pastry box onto the table. Her hands shook as she lifted the lid. Inside sat the most beautiful ring she had ever seen. A single diamond surrounded on each side by a ruby that had been encased in gold scrollwork. "It's—" Words failed her. She was afraid to speculate what the ring might mean. She was afraid to breathe for fear that she might be dreaming. Finally she mustered the strength to look at Nathaniel.

He took her free hand then got down on one knee next to the couch.

"Trixie, we've known each other for almost a decade. When you left, six years ago I was deeply hurt." He held his hand up to stop her from interrupting. "It was as if someone had turned off the light in my life. So I left. And when I returned, your life had changed and quite frankly, so had mine. But when I found you in that file room I realized the things that mattered most, hadn't changed."

She sniffled back tears. "What things would those be?"

"Like the way your eyes light up when you describe something you are passionate about." He tipped his head toward the table. "Or the way you savor every single morsel of those pastries. And the way you stand by the people you love, no matter what."

He took a deep breath. "I know we only spent a few days together while we searched for Peter, but I want you to know how much those days meant to me. Some people in polite society might say that because we spent so much time together in private that we should be forced to wed." Once again, he held up his hand to halt her objections. "Quite frankly, I don't give a damn what those people say. I'm here, on my knee because I want to be. Because I spent the last three weeks without you by my side and I find that I don't want to spend another day like that."

A tear rolled down her cheek.

"I love you Trixie. I always have. I always will. I want you with me through thick and thin. Through sickness and health." He took the box from her hand, removed the ring, and held it out for her. "Will you do me the honor of standing by my side for the rest of my life and becoming my wife?"

Her lip quivered but she nodded. "Yes. I can think of nothing more I would rather do than to spend every day from now to eternity with you."

He closed the distance between them and sealed their affirmations with a kiss. When he pulled away they were both grinning like fools.

He slipped the ring on her finger. "The jeweler said he could fit it to any size we needed."

"It's perfect. I love it." She looked up at him.

"And I love you."

"I love you, too."

"Our marriage won't interfere with your work with the RIO, will it?" She bit her lip, almost afraid of his answer.

"Some." He touched her lip and smiled. "Instead of a lonely bachelor on the prowl, I'll have the perfect cover as a happily married man traveling with his beautiful wife on his arm. Invitations to events will be far easier to obtain."

"So does that mean I will go with you on missions?"

He kissed her. "Anywhere I go, you go. But I will never allow you to be placed in danger."

"That's all I ask." She kissed him back.

Never in a million years could she have imagined that she would here —with her mother, father, and her brother just down the hall, safe and sound— and that the man she loved, loved her in return despite her quirks and disregard of social norms. But, oh, how she looked forward to a lifetime of love and adventure.

THE END

If you enjoyed this book, please consider leaving a review!

EXCERPT

Margaret Ingleton is a gently bred young lady who inadvertently puts herself and the man she loves in danger while helping her brother fulfil his mission for the Royal Intelligence Office.

Turn the page to read an excerpt from *To London, With Love.*

1

"AND *that* is why I rarely bother letting mother know when I come back to Carlisle," Colin Stanbury grumbled as he hurried back to the shipping docks. After spending more than an hour listening to endless suggestions about how to find a suitable wife, his mother had proceeded to review her list of possible candidates. Out of all of the ladies she listed, the one name he gave a damn about still didn't make the cut.

Margaret Ingleton.

Even though Margaret was daughter of one of his mother's closest friends, Baroness Ingleton, it had never been deemed a good match. He might be the third son to a Viscount, but that didn't mean he was worthy.

But that was old news.

At least he'd managed to hear how the rest of the family fared before the boring part started.

He glanced at his watch again. He needed to get back to his airship quickly if he was to make his next delivery on time. Unfortunately, his bum knee bothered him today and he hadn't taken the time to properly lubricate the gears in his mechanical brace before leaving London. His limp was even more pronounced as he hurried back to the docks.

Being a pilot for Panhurst Air Company might seem like menial work but he loved it. It involved very little physical labor since dockworkers managed the on and off loading of goods. Not that he minded getting his hands dirty. Sometimes he pitched in when they were shorthanded. His genteel upbringing and his friendship with Peter, one of the company owners, put him in a position to deliver valuable, easily stolen items like jewels or important documents.

The frequent travel satisfied his wanderlust and his need to get away from his mother's constant interference. How either of his older brothers remained at Rockcliffe, the family estate, and stayed sane, he'd never know.

When he finally reached the docks, he checked in with the dock master to ensure everything had been prepared while he'd been away.

"Aye. Williams and Sons picked up the shipment about quarter after." The dock master reported. "We refueled *The Windsail* and checked her lines. Everything reported in satisfactory condition. You're good to go. Just check in with the office for a launch time."

"Will do." Colin tipped his hat. "Thanks."

"Oh, one more thing," the dock master's shout stopped him short. "There was a young lady looking for you."

"A young lady?" Colin frowned. "Did she give a name?"

"No. Right proper thing. I sent her to the office to keep her off the docks."

Colin gestured that he'd heard and headed toward the office. Who would come looking for him here? Only Panhurst and his mother knew he would be in town.

He checked in at the desk and asked about the lady, but they indicated no one had come looking for him. Shrugging it off as a mistake, he obtained his launch time then headed to *The Windsail*.

He completed his usual checks of the ship then settled in his chair to wait.

Despite his efforts to block it out, his mother's voice echoed in his head. He was wasting his life flying around in a balloon. He wasn't getting any younger. He needed to settle down, marry, and provide them with grandchildren to dote on.

Why was she harping on him? He had two older brothers for that.

He'd come to the conclusion long ago that any woman who

satisfied his mother's requirements as a wife would never make him happy. So why bother? Besides, what woman would want a man who was half crippled?

He checked his pocket watch. Five minutes until launch. He flipped the switch on the engine to heat the air in the balloon. The rope net encasing the balloon creaked as the gray fabric stretched. According to Peter, the increased temperature enabled the ship to rise.

He and Peter Wadeworth had been at university together. The science behind airship travel had always fascinated Peter. So much that he designed two of the company's newest ships, including *The Windsail*. Colin preferred the mechanical aspects of the ship engines. He also liked being able to make repairs when things went awry without waiting for help.

When he received his signal from the dock master, Colin adjusted the dials and levers on the control desk and slowly navigated *The Windsail* up and away.

Take off was always a moment of tension and exhilaration. There were dozens, if not hundreds, of things that could go wrong with a launch. But you couldn't beat the view of the city shrinking away below.

As soon as he reached the height he wanted, he leveled out the ship and checked his compass against his maps. Normally it would take a couple of hours to reach Liverpool, but if he burned a little extra fuel in the propeller now he could make up the time he lost because of his mother.

He rechecked his calculations then he settled into the captain's chair to wait for his marker to turn off the propeller. As soon the engine stopped, blessed quiet filled the cabin. He reached for the jug of coffee he brought and poured some into a mug. He barely got his second sip down when he heard something move in one of the storage cabinets.

Damn. If that last shipment had mice in it, he was going to say something to Devadas about checking crates better. It took two of the dock cats almost three weeks to get rid of the last infestation. He didn't want to lose *The Windsail* for that long again.

He jerked open the door to one cabinet and looked inside. It was relatively empty and there were no droppings or shredded material indicating mice had burrowed inside. He popped open the next compartment and searched. Still no sign of mice.

When he opened the third door, he fell back in surprise. "What the—"

"Now don't be angry," Margaret Ingleton pleaded from her hiding place.

"Don't be angry?" He grabbed her by the arms and pulled her out of the closet with little finesse and probably more force than needed but he accomplished the task without hurting either of them. "I should take you over my knee right now for stowing away on my ship! What the deuces is wrong with you?" God she smelled good. How long had it been since he'd last seen her?

She shot him a look of annoyance as she straightened her skirt. A few locks of her blond hair had slipped lose. She pushed them back into place. Even after riding in a cramped cabinet she was still beautiful enough to make him ache.

Without releasing his hold of her, he narrowed his gaze. "You were the woman who asked for me at the dock, weren't you?"

She tried to look innocent, but nodded.

He let go and paced away from her. If he didn't, he was either going to throttle her or kiss her. Neither were good options. "Our ships are watched. How did you get aboard without our people seeing you?"

She opened her mouth but he cut her off by throwing both hands up in the air in a gesture of pure frustration. "And why?"

"I—"

He paced toward the other side of the cabin. "Does your mother know where you are?"

"She—"

He shook his head. "Of course she doesn't. She would never allow her daughter to go gallivanting off to the shipping yard." He pointed at her. "And she certainly wouldn't let you sneak aboard a ship that you only hoped belonged to someone you knew."

"But I—"

His stomach sank. "Dear God, what if you had gotten on the wrong ship. Do you know what could have happened to you?"

"Well, that—"

"Nothing good!" He prided himself on not shaking some sense into her right then and there. He stomped to the other side of the cabin. "This ship is headed for Liverpool. What is so important that you risked not only your virtue and reputation, but possibly your life, to go to Liverpool? Tell me," he bellowed.

She folded her arms over her chest. "I will if you will stop yelling at me long enough to answer."

He wiped his hand down his face. Did this woman have no sense of self-preservation? No wonder her brothers frequently complained about her when they were youths. "Tell me. Please," he said with far more calm and patience than he really possessed.

"I need to go to London."

"London? Why didn't you take the train or have Lucas take you by coach?"

She shook her head. "It wasn't possible."

He held up one hand. "Let me guess. Lucas told you he wasn't wasting his time or coin on whatever you were scheming?"

"No, he's busy with a…" She looked away. "…a situation at home. It wasn't possible for him to leave."

"Couldn't your mother escort you to London? Surely she wouldn't mind a few days in the city."

"She refused to leave Jake."

He stopped pacing and faced her. "Jake? I thought he was overseas."

"He was but he…" She clasped her hands together. "He returned earlier this week. Unfortunately, he had a bit of an accident on the way home."

He raised one brow. "What kind of accident?"

"He was shot."

Colin reared back. "He was shot? What happened?"

"We don't really know. Lucas has been trying to figure it all out."

"Where was he shot?"

"In one of the nearby farmer's field."

Colin rolled his eyes. "No, I meant where on his body was he injured?"

"Oh, yes. He was shot twice. Once in the head and once in the leg."

"In the head? And he's alive?" Her story was getting harder to believe.

"Yes, thankfully. The doctor said he was lucky that the bullet only grazed the side of his head. His leg however is going to be some time healing."

"That was lucky. I'm sorry to hear about Jake." He crossed his arms over his chest. "But that still doesn't explain why you think you need to go to London so urgently. Especially when your brother, who has been away for more than a year, is home and injured. This smells fishy to me."

She lifted her chin. "It does pain me to have to leave Jake, but there is a private matter I need to attend to and it simply cannot wait."

He narrowed his gaze. "What kind of private matter."

"The very definition of private implies that one doesn't want to discuss the matter with anyone."

He leaned against the captain's desk. "Well it seems to me that you're stuck between a rock and a hard place because I have heard nothing that makes me want to take you anywhere except Blackford Manor."

~ Look for *To London, With Love* at your favorite book retailer ~

ABOUT THE AUTHOR

Dena Garson is an award-winning author of contemporary, paranormal, fantasy, and sci-fi romance. She holds a BBA and a MBA in Business and works in the wacky world of quality and process improvement. Making up her own reality on paper is what keeps her sane.

She is the mother of two rowdy boys and two rambunctious cats (AKA the fuzzy jerks) When she isn't writing you can find her at the sewing machine or stringing beads. She is also a devoted Whovian and Dallas Cowboys fan.

Find Dena on the web at:

Website - http://www.denagarson.com/
Facebook - https://www.facebook.com/AuthorDenaGarson
Twitter - https://twitter.com/DenaGarson
Email – Dena@DenaGarson.com

OTHER BOOKS BY DENA GARSON

Steampunk
Christmas Royale
To London, With Love

Paranormal/Fantasy/Sci-Fi Romance
Ghostly Persuasion
Mystic's Touch
Rege's Rescue
Vordol's Vow
When Ash Remains
Who Wants Forever
Your Wild Heart

Contemporary Romance
Down to Business
Loss of Control
Risky Business
Snow Effect

Short Stories (Contemporary)
Cherie's Silk
Working It All Out

Find detailed information on all of Dena's books at:
http://www.denagarson.com/books.html

www.ingramcontent.com/pod-product-compliance
Lightning Source LLC
Chambersburg PA
CBHW020958180626
46814CB00003B/1159